The Fourteenth Colony

A NOVEL WITH MUSIC

THE FOURTEENTH COLONY

by Jason T. Lewis

This book is a work of fiction.

Special thanks to Michael Reynnells and all those who
supported this publication through kickstarter.com.

This edition was created through the hard work and support
of many friends, including Gerry Schramm, David Etler,
and Anna Kreuger.

To download the companion album
visit www.sadironpress.com

ALBUM CREDITS:

All songs written by Jason T. Lewis

Performed by:
      Jason T. Lewis: Vocals, guitars, auxiliary percussion
      Randall Davis: Guitars, lap steel
      Ryan Bernemann: Bass, vocals, accordion
      Adam Bernemann: Drums
      Brian Umlah: Trumpet on "Back in Town"

Produced by Randall Davis and Jason T. Lewis
Recorded at Flat Black Studio, Iowa City and Sad Iron Studio, Iowa City
Mixed by Pete Becker
Mastered by Carl Saff

For Theresa and Vaughan

Dedicated to my father

The hum of the amp. Feel it through the floor, hollow plywood stage, boots sticking to beer-tacky carpet, once green, or grey, now dark sea of stain. Loop the strap overhead. The weight of hard wood tethering you to the stage but you are ready to fly, fingers tingling, heart pounding. Alive. This is what it is to be alive. Feel the strings, tripwires; plectrum, vibration, wood and steel, magnetic coils, electricity, amplifier, speak, sound explosion. Alchemy. An open mouth on a puckered wound, sucking the poison out. The vessel that will carry the voice. Wait, mouth closed, feel the words tickling the throat, the pressure building inside, like a heart attack must feel, but beautiful, coveted death explosion. Then rebirth. You are the shell that protects the voice, cocoon to chrysalis, vessel to ancient incantation. The voice has always been, the vessel had to be molded from fleshclay. Three years old, the voice took over; powerful, so much power. How could anything that harnessed that power ever be struck down? The more you used it, the more powerful the voice became, until there was nothing of the vessel. You were the voice. It consumed you. It consumed everything you set in its way.

There were lies you invented yourself and the voice said them back to you. Echolalia.

Feel the hum. The voice bubbling up. Feet on the plywood, gently buoyant under your weight. The plectrum cold, soon to be warmed by friction. Don't strum too hard. Let the tool do the work. Pluck the chord like the strap of a thin chemise slipping from a shoulder. The first assent. And the first loss.

CHAPTER 1

The school was for sale. A dingy, tilted realtor sign, pockmarked and faded, stood sentinel in the small patch of grass where we kids used to board the buses. "Price reduced!" said the sign.

I let the van coast as I came even with the old building. How many days had I spent in there—first grade to eighth—hundreds, maybe thousands? God, I hated that place, the smell of chalk dust, the feel of it bloating my hands as I sweat at the board struggling to diagram a sentence, or solve some equation; the overheated rooms, the overcooked food, the paddling I took in the principal's office when I called Mrs. Wenzel a bitch—fifth grade, a year or so after Mom and Dad split up, after it sank in that the split was permanent. The principal had an over-wet mouth; white, foamy spittle collected in the corners. He sat me in his office and looked me up and down. It was an elaborate show, one that I'm sure he'd worked out over the years and polished to perfection. *That kind of talk is not acceptable in school and to use a word like that directed at a teacher is inexcusable.* He bent me over his desk and whacked me three times with his fraternity paddle. I didn't cry. I didn't whimper. I took it and it hurt, but I wasn't going to let him make me cry.

God, I hated that place. And now it was for sale, price reduced.

I couldn't just pass by. I had to stop and look. I pulled into the far side of the turnabout. The van's frame groaned over the rumpled pavement. It was only a matter of time before the van collapsed on me, but it had gotten me across the country, been a hotel and a refuge on four tours, and now it had gotten me home.

I idled before the steps and studied the crumbling brick façade, the weathered sandstone columns flanking the doors, the peeled white paint, the broken windows. How long had the place been empty? I fought the urge to get out of the van and throw chunks of asphalt through the remaining panes of glass. A coal truck geared down and rolled by slow. I was untethered. The past and the present existing on the same plane. Further down the road, the coal truck grumbled as it started the climb out of town, heading out the way I'd come.

Thirteen years. When I last saw these streets I was eighteen years old, riding high in the back seat of a Greyhound bus. I was too young to know that you never sit in the backseat of a Greyhound, to avoid the perverts and the smell from the toilet. I still can't stand the smell of that blue liquid they use in those things. As the bus rolled by the school on the way out of town I wasn't thinking about anything but the world of possibility that awaited me. I gave the school the finger through the tinted window and felt satisfied. I had my cheap second-hand guitar, a suitcase of all the wrong clothes and three hundred dollars I'd gotten for graduating high school. I didn't tell anyone I was leaving. I was afraid if I told anyone and they looked at me wrong I'd lose my nerve. And I needed to get out. My life depended on it. Now I was sneaking back into town, shamed, broken, angry, the same as when I left.

I couldn't look at the school anymore. I decided it was the saddest thing I ever saw in my life. The urge to turn back and follow the coal truck out of town was strong, but the few dollars in my pocket and the fact I had nowhere else to go were stronger.

I hadn't spoken to my mother in four years, when I called her on her birthday after I got drunk enough to dial the number. I sat by the phone, downing beer after beer, watching the day die through a motel window, trying to put my hand on the phone. I was afraid she'd hang up on me, but when I finally dialed the number and said, "Hey Mom," she cried.

"Are you coming home?" she said through the sobs. There was the crunckle of a beer can against the receiver and I knew she had to be as drunk as me, celebrating in her same old way. I lied and said I'd come home soon, maybe that summer, maybe the next Christmas, but back then I had no intention of ever coming back. I listened to her talk, blubbering over how much she missed me. When she started in with stories about people that I didn't want to remember I hurried off the phone with a happy birthday and a spine-shivering "I love you." I never called again. Now I drove through town girding myself for the welcome she might have for me, maybe with open arms, maybe with a door slamming in my face, maybe just a few tears and then we'd pretend like I'd never left.

The "downtown" area was just one street, Front Street, three blocks long that ran between the railroad tracks and Route 7. Angled toward the road at the intersection where you turned to get to Front Street, the local Moose Lodge had posted a sign in the time since I left. It looked like something stolen from a national park, varnished logs and hand-carved lettering, painted gold and green, the high school colors. It read: *Vandalia, W.Va.—Where business meets pleasure*. It was clear there was neither business nor pleasure in Vandalia. Next to the sign was a wrought iron marker that identified our town as the last symbol of the aborted fourteenth colony of Vandalia. We learned about it in school, how the borders were surveyed and the capital chosen, but then the Revolutionary War broke out and by the time it was over, Vandalia had been forgotten. It was part of West Virginia history class in the eighth grade. Every once in a while I would mention it in conversation, but no one ever knew what I was talking about. No one had ever heard of the fourteenth colony. But then again, usually when I told someone where I grew up they said something like, "Oh yeah? I have a friend who lives in Roanoke."

I didn't remember town this way, half dead, broken down. I rode down Front Street and surveyed the wasteland; the supermarket, new not long before I left, the windows now caked with road grime, the paint peeling from the sign I remembered as bright and fresh. The library was shuttered, a window display of children's books furry with dust. The storefront where Dad bought me a baseball glove I never used was long empty, fall leaves blown against the door. Next door to that, the historical society in the building that used to be the courthouse, pictures in the windows of black-faced miners, the old hospital in the years when it was a TB asylum. In another window, a diorama of quilts, railroad spikes, a butter churn, a miner's helmet, a musket, and the state flag.

Front Street might have been the official downtown, but the real town center was about a half mile down the road where several of the older streets in town converged on Route 7 to make a lopsided triangle. On one corner of the triangle was Howdy's service station (the owner's last name was Howdershelt, but everyone called him Howdy), catty-corner to Howdy's was the Dipsie Doodle, and the point of the triangle was the pharmacy on one side of the road and the bank on the other. This triangle was where all the business in town got done. When I was small, Dad took me to Howdy's late on Saturday mornings. Howdy always let me go behind the counter and pick out a candy bar, which he'd let me work off by emptying the garbage cans into the dumpster in the back. If Howdy's was still standing there was hope. But it wasn't. The windows were boarded over, the gas pumps gone, exposed pipes laced with yellow caution tape.

Across the road, the Dipsie Doodle was renamed the Hog Pen, although nothing had really changed about it except there was a Harley Davidson sign in the window. I couldn't help but scan the parking lot for a truck that could have been Dad's. The Doodle was Dad's second favorite bar after the VFW. He went to the Doodle in the second half of the month, when he'd run up too much of a tab at the VFW. If he had a really bad month, he'd continue down the road to Stoney's, but that place was almost to the Maryland border and you had to drive through town to get there from the cabin. It wasn't a good idea to end a long day of drinking with a drive through town. But Dad did it anyway.

Any one of the trucks in the Hog Pen lot could have been his, all beat down, rusted out, not a single one manufactured after 1989. There were a couple motorcycles in the lot. I wasn't ready for a place like that. It was still early and I couldn't be sure I wanted to find Dad, if he was here to find. I hadn't spoken to him in more than half my life, he was no more father to me than a tree stump, whatever influence he'd once had over me was long gone. I decided a long time ago that I hated him. Maybe I blamed him for things, but in a more honest moment I couldn't say it was all him that made things turn out like they did. After a while he became like a memory of a movie I'd seen a long time ago.

My old neighborhood was no improvement over the rest of the town. The old houses in the nicer section I remembered as majestic were chalky white aluminum-sided four squares, eaves rotting, curtain-less windows. I once thought this part of the neighborhood was where the rich people lived. Seeing these sad, old places, I don't know how I got that idea.

When I was a kid, this was a decent middle class neighborhood, lots of families, some older folks, but a good place to grow up. There was a school and a playground nearby, not too many cars on the roads and what cars there were drove slow and careful through the streets. It was the kind of neighborhood where we kids played touch football in the road until the streetlights came on. I remember those early years, when I was really young, as nice, quiet. As I got older the neighborhood started to change. The more upwardly mobile families moved out to the new developments near the lake or out of town altogether. The families who had found their level, mine included, stayed longer, but most trickled away. By the time I was in high school there were no more kids my age left in the neighborhood, just old people and rentals. Not that I cared all that much by then. I was never really a part of any group. I was the kid who the rest of the kids never called for basketball games or when they were going to build an ice fort on a snow day. I was the kid who sat in the picture window, surveying the neighborhood until I saw signs of activity on a yard a few houses away, or a group of kids dribbling a ball toward the playground and then I would race to put my sneakers on, feet pounding, heartbroken and running after them.

I turned the corner to the old house, girding myself for a shock, but the street in the dusk looked so different that I thought I made a wrong turn. The old man who owned the land at the end of the road had a huge garden and beyond that a small copse of trees that most of the kids who never spent any time out in the county mistook for woods. It was our fort, our jungle, later the place where I first kissed a girl. It was the place I went to hide when Mom and Dad fought. There was a huge stand of boxwood, hollow on the inside, that I stayed in for hours while I waited for things to cool down, or I saw Dad drive away in his truck.

But the woods were gone, along with the old man's garden, and half of the houses on the side of the street opposite ours, replaced by cheap-looking tan row houses. Our house was still there though, still the same, if not a little shabbier. Relief. Moments before I'd been dreading the sight of it, not wanting to knock on that door, see Mom's face, explain myself, or worse—not having to explain myself and her with welcoming arms. Now I was just happy that the place still existed.

I parked across the street in front of the first row of condos and looked the place over. Not much had changed; the siding was still tan, the eaves still white, paint peeling, but the house looked smaller, a little cracker box of a ranch sitting at the top of a little slope. The picture window still there—lens of Christmas mornings' snow, birds on the telephone wire, college girls stepping from the shower in the rental house that was gone now, a brief glimpse of skin in the morning light before school. The house was and was not the house of my memory, but instead a dingy little two bedroom, porch railings rusted, mailbox dangling by one screw, fiberglass garage door dirty, streaked window pane in the picture window frame. I sat for a few minutes more. No lights on. Full dark came. The sodium street lamps flickered to life, casting their piss-yellow pall across the dash, giving my fingers, still white-knuckled on the wheel, jaundice. I had to do it.

The flagstone steps had come loose of their mortar and I walked along the edges of the stairs to keep from slipping. It was cold. It had been a while since I'd been in a winter, how the cold got into your blood, and I realized my jean jacket was not going to be enough. A wind rolled down the hill and cut through me.

I came even with the curtain-less picture window and ventured a peek inside. I couldn't make out anything—no furniture, no shapes whatsoever—then came a thunder from inside. A dog. A big dog. I took a step back. I've hated big dogs since I was small. A family one street down had a Siberian husky that took a chunk out of my thigh one afternoon when I was playing tag with the other kids. I still have the image of the dog leaping up and his mouth clamped onto my thigh. Mom raised a stink and called the cops, who insisted that the dog get checked for rabies. I still have the scar on my thigh from that bite.

A huge German shepherd crashed into the glass. The pane wanted to give, bowed out from the force, but it held and the dog threw itself into it over and over again, spittle flying from its jowls. From somewhere deep in the house: "Get the fuck down, you piece of shit." A man's voice. A voice I didn't recognize. The dog kept on coming, clawing at the window. I could see now the wooden sill was nearly scraped away from similar incidents.

Footsteps inside the house pounding toward the window. The dog backed off at their approach. Somewhere inside the dark room, a smack, a whimper, and the dog was gone into the house. Back toward the bedrooms, a door slammed. The man returned.

"Who the fuck are you?" I couldn't see the person speaking, somewhere inside the room outside the light that spilled in from the street lamps.

"This is my house," I said.

"The fuck it is. This my house. I've been in this house going on two years, fucking crackhead. Get the fuck out of here before I call the law."

My mom wasn't the kind of person who left. She was the kind of person who talked about leaving, but never did. She would never have sold the house. I knew that.

"This was my house," I said. "I grew up here. My mom lives here." I was regressing to some kind of child-like state, the pitch of my voice higher, pleading.

"Oh shit." The voice softened a little, lowered in volume. The ghost of a shape moved past the window. The heavy wooden door opened. "Come in here."

I entered my childhood home. The room was still dark and the dog started up again somewhere in the house, my old bedroom, it sounded like.

"I apologize," the man said. His voice was soft now. It was a black man's voice. When I was a kid there were no blacks in Vandalia. He turned on a lamp. Before me was a man in his middle forties, maybe five foot eight, stocky, with a pot belly. He was wearing a maintenance uniform from the hospital. I knew it was a maintenance uniform because Dad wore the same one when he worked there. The shirt was open, white T-shirt underneath. The name over his left breast: Harold. "You want something to drink?" Harold said.

I looked at him for a few seconds, confused. "Where's my mom?"

He looked at the floor.

I knew then she was dead.

"I'll get you a Coke," he said. "Sit down." He went to the kitchen and I stood in the little foyer waiting, shivering. He came back with two Diet Cokes, opened them both and handed one to me.

He said, "Shit," looked at me, then took a long drink. "Come sit down." He waved me to an armchair across the room. He looked me in the eye, like he was trying to see something. "The lady that lived here—your mother—died two years ago. Drunk driving accident."

I was sick. I swallowed hard to keep the bile down. I took a drink of the Coke. It was hard to draw a breath. "She was drunk?"

"No. No. Some high school kid. Football Friday, drunk as a skunk. Walked away without a scratch. Sad thing. I never go out when there's a football game. Those kids are like animals these days."

We were quiet for a minute. The dog scraped at a door down the hall. The furnace kicked on. I couldn't speak. Harold went back into the kitchen to give me some time alone. I could hear him in there, moving around, not knowing what to do with himself. I looked out the picture window for a long time, trying to recognize anything at all. I couldn't. The sun glowed pink beyond the hills, the color of blood and milk, but the valley was dark. I went out to the kitchen.

"I'm sorry I bothered you. I didn't know. I hadn't talked to her in a few years."

"It's OK." Harold was making a sandwich. He worked the midnight shift at the hospital. I woke him up with my arrival. He spread mayonnaise on white bread and I slipped in time, seeing Mom do the same thing hundreds of times in the same exact spot. I could almost taste the white bread. He slipped the sandwich into a baggie and dropped it into a soft, insulated lunch bag.

He said, "I saved some things that were still in the house. Funny, I feel like I know you. There were all these papers in a box in the basement, old school papers and stuff. I couldn't help but look. You get curious to want to know who lived in your house before you. You can go look if you want to. The closet under the stairs. Take them if you want."

I hesitated.

"Go on, I've got a while before I have to go to work." Harold said. "It's OK."

When Mom and Dad bought the house, the basement was unfinished. Before Dad left, the basement became the family room. After Dad left, it was my bedroom. He renovated it himself with hand-hewn cherry wood paneling. He laid thin low-pile carpet over the concrete floor (green and brown with a fleur-de-lis pattern) and brought in a couple beanbag chairs and a couch, a TV, of course. I kept all my toys down there in the same closet where Harold had shoved the box containing the remains of my childhood. One of my earliest childhood memories was watching TV using Dad's butt as a pillow. We watched a lot of variety and musical revue shows: The Captain and Tennille, Sonny and Cher, Donny and Marie, Lawrence Welk, "Hee Haw." Those were good times, before the late-night fighting, before Dad stayed out all night drinking.

I descended the stairs in the dark, afraid to turn the lights on and see the room entirely. I felt my way to the closet and found the pull string for the light, right where it was the last time I used it. I knew the box right away; a huge old hat box I found in my grandmother's attic when I was seven or eight. It was round and gold, the box I used to store anything from the ticket stub I got when Mom took me to Disney World, newspaper clippings of Pirates box scores from the early eighties, to a drawing I made of Spider-Man and love notes that were passed to me from desk to desk in junior high, every paper artifact of my young life. I saved everything.

I pulled the box out of the closet and picked the first relic off the top—a program from a choir concert when I was in the second grade. I remembered it in a rush of senses, the dusty hot smell of the gym, my sweating palms, the footlights blinding me to the crowd beyond the stage, the way my heart murmured as I walked to the mic for my solo. Beneath the program, the lyrics to the first song I tried to write. I read the first lines and flushed red. Terrible. Embarrassing. I couldn't look further into the box, not yet. Harold walked across the floor upstairs and for a second I thought Mom was coming. But she wasn't. She wouldn't. I sat cross-legged on the floor, the light from the closet spilling into my lap and held my face in my hands.

A year or so after the divorce Mom started dating again. I was nine or ten. I didn't like it. I hoped that maybe she and Dad would get back together. She never dated any one guy for too long and for a while I thought that meant there was still hope. The guys were always forty-ish and single, misfits and nerds, friends of friends. Most of these guys looked at me like a dead spot in an otherwise fine-looking patch of lawn. And that was OK. I didn't want anything to do with them either. They took Mom to the Owl's Club for dinner and then later I listened to them groping on the couch. I stayed awake to make sure Mom didn't get in trouble. Usually, the guy gave up after a half hour or so and she showed him the door. I was proud of her. I thought she was getting stronger. Until Stan.

Stan was an all-right guy for the most part. He sold insurance and had a new car. He used to drive a cab in Morgantown and had all kinds of crazy stories about people he'd driven from place to place—a guy who called him when his wife stabbed him with a steak knife. In the middle of winter and the guy came out of his trailer shirtless with the knife sticking out of his chest. It had gone deep enough that the serrated edge was stuck in his ribs, but not deep enough to puncture anything important. The wife followed the guy outside screaming, "You come back here again and I'll carve you up, motherfucker." Stan laughed his head off every time he told the story.

Stan was pretty nice to me. He played football in high school, listened to ZZ Top and loved professional wrestling. Stan started staying overnight after a few months, only on weekends. The rest of the time he lived across the county with his mother. That should have been a warning sign, but at the time I was just glad to have someone to hang out with who seemed to like me. We'd watch wrestling together on Saturday mornings and even though I knew it was fake and thought it was stupid it was nice to have a guy to do stuff with. Stan treated me like a buddy.

Mom was happy with him at first, too, and that made me glad. In those first couple years after Dad left, she went from relieved that he was gone, listening to radio stations he never liked, planting tomato plants in the side yard, to sitting in the living room the day after a date went bad and smoking, not talking. When she met Stan it seemed like everything might get back to normal, that maybe we'd be able to be a family, but Stan was a drinker and he didn't only drink beer, like Dad; he was a whiskey man.

Until Stan, I don't remember Mom ever drinking. Stan was uncomfortable around people who wouldn't do the same things as he did. They fought about it late at night, Stan sloppy drunk and Mom trying to steer him into bed. At first, he was a jovial drunk, he kidded her about it but after a while he got mean. He called her a frigid bitch. He said she was judging him. She was lonely and Stan was the first good thing that happened to her in a long time. Soon she started coming home as drunk as he was, if not worse.

And Stan could confine his drinking to the weekends. He'd drink, puke, get up and do it again the next day, but when Monday rolled around, he was freshly scrubbed and chipper, ready to hit the road and sell some insurance.

Mom didn't handle herself as well. It wasn't long before she was buying forties to put herself to sleep at night when Stan was across the county. Those nights, Mom sat on the couch in front of the TV, sucking on her forty until she was tired enough to go to sleep. That's about when I started sleeping in the basement. It was like having my own apartment. I put my mattress on the floor in the back corner of the room where I could watch TV or read until I went to sleep. I could come and go through the garage door, piss in the basement shower and wash and dry my own clothes.

The only time I had to go upstairs was for food and to take a crap. For a while it worked out OK.

Then Stan left Mom for another woman. He just didn't come to dinner one Friday night and Mom knew what was going on. I heard her on the phone, talking to his mother, yelling after the woman hung up on her. She stomped around upstairs. The ashtray by the couch clanked on the end stand, cigarette after cigarette stubbed out. She downed a couple forties on the couch, enough to really get her buzzed. I almost went upstairs to try and talk to her, but I heard her talking to herself, cursing, and that scared me a little. Then she left without saying anything to me. She was gone a few hours. I read for a while, watched a movie, tried not to think about her, but it was hard. Around one, I heard the car pull in the driveway, the front door open, uneven footsteps across the floor. The radio came on, blasting out the Top 40 station.

I pulled the covers up to my ears. I could tell she was really drunk by how many times she stumbled into furniture and cursed. I curled into a ball. She ran into every object in the house on her way to the bedroom. Maybe she would just pass out. . . . No. She thumped around the bedroom, still talking to herself. She made her way into the kitchen. The refrigerator opened, closed, and then she opened and closed it again. *Just steer yourself to bed*, I said to myself.

The basement door opened and from where I lay in bed I saw her bare feet and legs begin their descent.

"I want a hot dog," she said in a sing-songy voice, like she was cheering for the home team at a football game. I played possum, eyes half-closed.

"I wanna hot dog, Hi-dee-ho!" She said it louder this

time. When I didn't respond she kept saying it, stumbling down a step or two each time. At first, I saw her bare legs and thought she was in the baggy old T-shirt she wore as a nightie. But as she chanted her mantra, first her calves, then thighs, bare hips, waist, and finally breasts, pendulous and dangling, descended into the basement.

At the bottom she said, "I want a hot dog, Hi-dee-ho!"

I didn't respond.

"You fucker, I want a hot dog."

"Go to bed, Mom."

"Don't tell me what the hell to do. I want a hot dog."

I couldn't look at her.

"We don't have any hot dogs," I said.

"Don't tell me that." She was breathing hard, and her speech was thick, like she was talking through two fat lips.

"Where's Stan?" I asked.

"I need a hot dog," she said quietly. She had started to cry. She sat down hard on the steps, put her head between her knees, and threw up. Spit trailed from her lips.

"Why doesn't anyone want to love me?" she said.

She lifted her hair above her head with one hand and wiped her mouth with the other. She had vomit running down the inside of her shins. It was all I could do to keep from puking myself.

When I was little, maybe five or six, she had a hysterectomy. I didn't know what that was, but knew it wasn't good. She came home from the hospital on a Friday afternoon. The next Monday she still couldn't get out of bed. I was late for school, Dad was already gone to work. I was standing by her bed, wondering what I should do, when she said, "Go into the living room and bring back your shoes." Her voice was weak, as it had been when she told me I would never have a brother or a sister, and I was too scared to ask why. I sat on the floor beside the bed, and she talked me through tying my shoes—bow, loop, pull through—over and over she said it. I forgot about school. It took me a long time to get it, but finally I did. She smiled at me when I was finished.

"You're such a big boy," she said. "I'm sorry you had to learn to do it this way. I am sorry. But I'm so proud of you."

It was the tenderest moment I can remember between us.

"I love you, Mom," I said, getting out of bed. I said it again as I made my way around the vomit at the bottom of the stairs. I lifted her by her armpits and guided her up the stairs to the bathtub where I rinsed her and pressed chunks down the drain with my fingertips. The smell of vomit mixed badly with the honeysuckle bath wash. More than once, I bent over the toilet, thinking I was going to be sick, but nothing came up.

"I'm sorry," she said. "I'm sorry, I'm sorry, I'm sorry, I'm sorry."

Her body was still damp when I tucked her into bed. Beneath her grogginess, she looked miserable and scared, but I forced myself to remember the way her face looked that day she taught me to tie my shoes.

She said, "I want a hot dog," one more time before she drifted off to sleep. I watched her face go slack, all the tension released.

I carried the box out of the basement and set it by the front door. The dog was finally quiet in the bedroom.

"You got some place to go?" Harold said. He looked at the clock. It would be time for his shift soon.

"I thought I did." I chuckled, to show him I was joking, but he didn't get my meaning. "I'll figure something out."

"Have you had supper? I made an extra sandwich."

"No, thanks. I should get going. You have to get to work soon."

"How do you know that?"

"My dad used to work the midnight shift at the hospital."

"Oh yeah? Who's that?"

I told him the name and he shook his head.

"No, can't say I know him, but that don't mean a lot."

"It was a long time ago."

We stood in the living room and I looked around. It was much the same as it had been when it was my house. Harold had hung pictures on the hooks where Mom hung pictures of me. A boy, a girl, maybe ten and twelve respectively. A woman. No Harold. He lived in this house alone. I wanted to ask where his family was, but didn't. What happened to Mom's old pictures? They weren't in the box.

He said, "I won't let you out of here until you sit and eat. You've just had a shock. You need to eat."

I was hungry. He led me to the table and I sat. He brought me the sandwich and put a bag of potato chips on the table, another can of Coke. I hadn't finished the first one, but I didn't say anything. He sat down beside me and pretended to look at the paper while I ate. The sandwich was thick-cut ham with American cheese and yellow mustard, white bread. Mom made me the same sandwich I don't know how many times. Everything was flowing together. I took the bread off the top and layered chips on top of the cheese. This was my favorite way to eat a sandwich when I was a kid. It had been years since I did that.

"You going to be all right?" Harold folded the paper and looked at me.

I shrugged.

"You need a place to stay you can stay here."

"You don't know me at all."

He laughed. "Feel like I do. Seems like you were quite the singer."

"Yeah."

"Still do it?"

"I did. Taking some time off. Waiting for new opportunities to develop."

"I hear that. Where were you living?"

"New York for a long time. Then LA."

He whistled. "Big time. You do anything I would have heard?"

"No."

"Well." He looked at the clock again.

"I better let you get to work," I said.

"I mean it. Stay here."

"Thanks, but I can't."

He offered to walk me to the van but I said no and thanked him again. He was trying to do something for me, but there was nothing more he could do. I went outside, box under my arm, still not quite accepting Mom was dead. I expected to see her at any moment in the picture window like I'd seen her a thousand times before, waving goodbye. Harold waved instead like he knew I was expecting it. I waved back.

CHAPTER 2

I told myself I would go straight to a motel, watch some TV and figure out my next move in daylight, but in the back of my mind I knew, so I wasn't surprised when I guided the car into the Hog Pen lot. I sat for a minute, watched the Harley sign flicker, and breathed deep, hoping for the strength to leave. I hadn't drank in a while. I didn't want to start again and I did. Three months sobriety down the drain, but it was a special occasion. Not every day you find out your mother died and you never knew it.

There used to be an old law on the books that you couldn't serve alcohol in town unless you were a private club. I think maybe that's why places like the Moose Lodge and the VFW were so popular. Maybe it had something to do with prohibition or maybe it was just the natural inclination of the people around here. I used to love going to bars with Dad, even though I knew he shouldn't be taking me to bars. Bars had jukeboxes, and pool tables, and fountain Cokes and I loved all three. What I loved even more was the feeling I got when we stood in front of the two-way mirror by the door and Dad let me hit the buzzer. I loved the feeling of walking through the door, everyone looking to see who we were, nodding, waving—we were welcome—and then going back to their beers.

The buzzer for the Dipsie Doodle was gone, only the bare wires wrapped in electrical tape remained. I fingered them for a second, wanting to press the buzzer and be accepted or rejected instead of having to walk into the place unannounced and take my chances. My heart was racing. My mouth watered for the first drink. I wanted it. I needed it. I hated myself with every molecule of my being. I grabbed the handle of the battered storm door and pushed through.

No one looked up when I entered. There was a klatch of guys at the far end of the bar, bathed in the blue-white glow of a TV set. The bartender stood behind the bar halfway between the door and the guys at the end. He whipped a dirty rag against the aluminum sink in front of him. Thunk—thunk—thunk, slow and mournful. He glanced at me when I came in but kept smacking the rag until I sat down on a stool close to the door.

My heart was pounding at this point, adrenaline pumping, three months of not drinking at the cusp of history. I was proud of myself for going that long without a drink. I'd thought it was a new start, but it was only a lull. The bartender approached and met my eyes, eyebrows raised, silently asking the question. He was younger than I thought at first, maybe forty and I thought maybe I should know him, but I didn't. *Order a Coke,* I told myself.

"What can I do you for?" The bartender spun the rag in front of him.

"Bud and a whiskey," I said.

"Any particular flavor?"

"Johnnie Walker Black?"

He shook his head. "That's a little above our pay grade."

"Beam."

I love to watch bartenders and witness their comfort in wielding such dangerous implements. I imagine that the guys who ran the guillotines had the same mundane calm about them after a while.

Beer and whiskey on the bar before me, neon winking

off the amber liquids, the bartender leaned back and crossed his arms. "I don't know you," he said.

I spun the whisky glass on the bar top, clockwise, counter-clockwise, like I was trying to unlock the combination of the trap I was about to fall into. I failed. The whiskey burned going down and I chased it with half the beer. My shoulders loosened, the familiar sliding down. "I grew up here," I said. "Just came back to town."

He nodded. I wanted to drink and not talk to anyone.

"You still got family around?" He wiped the aluminum top of the cooler in front of me, trying to seem uninterested, but I could tell he was interested, which made me a little nervous.

"I thought I did. I hadn't talked to my mom in a while. She died."

"Sorry to hear it." He poured me another whiskey and one for himself and we raised our glasses to Mom. He took a breath like he was going to say something else, but only patted the bar twice and went to refill the guys at the other end. He looked back at me as he went. One of the guys at the end hooked a thumb my way and the bartender shrugged.

The whiskey started to warm me up. My shoulders loosened more and my lips felt slack. It was a good feeling. I'd missed it. I took a long slug off the beer—cold, just the temperature it needed to be, holding somewhere just north of ice. This was the golden time, the reason I love to drink, the time before the next round or the round after made everything sloppy. If I could stay drunk like this forever I'd be happy.

There was a Mountaineer basketball game on TV. In New York, before I got too poor to own a TV, I watched the

Mountaineers any time I got the chance. It was the one way I stayed close to home. In high school I went to the games with Danny Fields, the only guy I'd say was my best friend. Maybe it's safe to say he was my only friend. Danny came to our school in the eighth grade after his family moved from Morgantown. He wore Hawaiian shirts, OP shorts and rope-soled beach shoes that first summer in band camp when everybody else was wearing Izod. He looked like a color-blind clown, but he was a pretty big guy for our age and could play basketball, so no one screwed with him. We both played in the drum section and neither of us were very good. That's how we became friends, lurking in the background hoping the director wouldn't notice we were barely keeping up with the parts. For all my musical talent, I never was much for practicing. Singing came easy, but the drums were work and I wouldn't do it, afraid I guess, that if I tried and failed then I had nowhere to hide.

Danny had a kind of magnetism to him. He wasn't like other guys. He had an earring—a tiny gold loop—and that was the first any of us saw of male ear fashion. Most of the guys were threatened by him and most of the girls were at least intrigued. He had a comfortable way with them that wasn't natural in most boys our age. He talked to girls in this low voice, almost a whisper that promised scenarios to make their parents lie awake nights worrying. And he was from the Big City: Morgantown, the place our parents took us to buy school supplies, where the University spread through the hills, bigger than anything we'd ever seen. By the end of summer band that year, Danny and I were inseparable and over the next few years we cut a path through the girls in our school, dating up the ladder until Danny stole away the head cheerleader from the captain of the football team. Holly Hawkins was all legs, hips, and a tsunami of permed hair. I called her The Claw because of the way her bangs loomed over her forehead, but never in front of Danny.

When Danny got his driver's license (Mom didn't let me get mine until I was seventeen and I'd taken driver's ed to get the insurance break) his mom bought him a Honda CRX, mostly to piss off his dad, who still lived in Morgantown and seemed to like that Danny was an hour away and not in his hair all the time.

Danny didn't seem to care about any of that. He went to see his dad when he needed twenty bucks and never lingered long. I studied him, wondering how he could stay so calm with everything falling apart around him.

We drove to Morgantown on game nights, telling our folks and our girlfriends we were going to study or something. We never studied. By that time I'd flunked out of every class I could to get into more music classes and Danny was never the sharpest tool in the shed. We'd go to the games, paying the six dollars to get in and we never watched a minute of the games, never even went to our seats. The high school girls in Morgantown went to the games but never sat in their seats, they went to the outer ring of the Coliseum and circled in packs to be ogled by boys like us. It wasn't long before Danny was dating a girl in Morgantown, too. I went along with him, told his lies and covered for him. We were friends.

Where was Danny Fields these days? Maybe still in town. What would I say, calling out of the blue? We drifted apart toward the end of school, the more I got into music and he got into Holly. *"Hey man, remember me? Yeah, it's been a long time. Hey listen, I'm in town, my Mom's dead and*

I just found out. I'm broke and I've got nowhere to sleep. You think I could crash on your couch?" Danny was the kind of guy that things came to without his trying. If he was still in town, he was probably married to some good-looking woman—maybe even Holly—living in a big house out by the lake, three kids that loved him even though he ignored them, making a lot of money as a restaurant owner or something. It was hard to bear the thought of him looking at me and seeing what I'd become, or hadn't become. I was the one who left for the big time, after all.

The bartender saw my half wave and came down the bar. I downed the rest of my drink as he approached. He refilled me without a word and took the money for the drinks from my change on the bar. I felt panicky, like I was falling and I couldn't grab a hold of anything to stop. As he walked away I said, "Hey man, you know a guy named Danny Fields?"

He put his hand on his head and rubbed it for a second, like he need help to get his memory working. After a second he said, "Nope. Should I?"

"No. He was a guy I used to know. My best friend in high school."

"Uh-uh. Sorry, man." He started to turn away.

"What about Ford Martin? He used to come in here a lot," I said.

He shook his head again. "I've only been working here six months, since the new owner. I don't know a lot of the old timers. He your dad?"

I nodded. "How'd you know?"

A shrug. "I figured you're working your way down a list."

Both of us watched the basketball game for a minute.

The team was good; a lot of ball movement, disciplined. There was one tall, goofy-looking kid, must have been almost seven-foot tall, who could drain the three from anywhere on the court. He knocked one down from the top of the key to put the Mounties up by a dozen and ran down the court, pounding on his chest with tattoo-covered arms, sweat glistening in the lights. A crowd shot, everyone going wild. Jesus H. Christ. Never saw anything like that when I was a kid.

The bartender put a phone book on the bar in front of me and patted it once before he walked away. I drank half my beer and flipped the book open. There he was: Daniel W. Fields. I traced my finger over the name a few times, not wanting to call, but knowing I would. I drank the rest of my drink. The other team was on a comeback. The Mounties were on the ropes. Tall, goofy hillbilly missed a long three. I was across the room punching Danny's number into the pay phone by the bathrooms. He picked up on the fourth ring.

"Motherfucker," he said after I stammered who I was. "I've been wondering what happened to you for ten years. I kept expecting to turn on the MTV and see you. What the hell's up, buddy?" He was so excited he almost stuttered. There was an edge to his voice.

"I don't know," I said, "just back in town for a little bit. Just got the thought to look you up in the phone book."

The guys at the bar yelled as the hillbilly missed another from downtown.

"Where are you right now?"

I told him.

"Don't move." The line went dead. I stood holding the receiver, not sure what happened. I went back to the bar.

While I waited, I worked up the courage to look in the M's. Dad's name nowhere to be found, but that didn't mean anything. It was likely that if he was in town, he didn't have a phone. Mom's name was still there, which sent a shiver up my spine. I checked the cover of the book. It was from the year she died.

I started crying, right there in the bar. I chewed on the inside of my lip to make it stop, but a fat tear rolled down my cheek and I just let it fall. If I wiped, the guys at the other end of the bar might see. I looked straight ahead into the mirror. My hair was too long and greasy. My face puffy, I could see the tracks of my tears in the dirt on my face. I'm surprised Harold let me into his house. I wouldn't have. The guy in the mirror was not the guy I thought I was. They say that you get a mental image of yourself at a certain age that stays in your mind's eye as your permanent visual of yourself. I think for me I see myself as twenty-five, thin, square shouldered, sallow-cheeked, mysterious. A joke. This wasn't the first time I looked in the mirror and didn't recognize the man looking back. Sometimes I scared myself, thinking there was a stranger in the room with me, when I caught a peek out of the corner of my eye. I studied the teary-eyed hobo in the mirror. Who was this pale, sunken-eyed bum? My T-shirt collar was brown with grime, stretched out and sagging. My jean jacket had a sheen from greasy hands. *This is who you are.* I turned away from the mirror. The basketball game was coming down to the last few minutes and the Mountaineers were still ahead, barely. I watched the game, waiting for Danny Fields to come and rescue me.

In the end, the Mountaineers lost a close one. The other team was too big, too strong, and they wore our boys down. The big hillbilly ended the game by hoisting a three that just rattled out. The two teams shook hands and walked off the court. The people in the stands sifted out of the arena and the camera stayed on a long shot of the empty floor. Two of the guys at the end of the bar got up and engaged in a listless game of pool. The bartender flipped a switch and the jukebox came to life: Foghat's "Slow Ride." I fell into watching the pool game, drank another whiskey and thought about putting quarters up for the next game. I was all warmed up now. Mom, coming back home, everything was receding into the rhythm of drunk.

"Lookatthissadsackmotherfucker." Danny wrapped me in a bear hug and squeezed. He was always a pretty big guy, but the arms that enclosed me were hard, bulging knots of muscle. I looked in the bar mirror and saw him, red-faced, vein bulging across his brow. His eyes were pinned. Coke? Meth? Steroids? All three? He released me just as I started to feel cartilage grind in my rib cage. I turned and smiled a fancy-meeting-you-here grin, playing it cool. He put both hands on my shoulders and turned me from side to side, checking me over. "So this is what a rock star looks like? I thought you'd be more glamorous-looking and less homeless-looking."

"This is the new fashion," I said. He looked me up and down again. He was so wired he was almost electrified.

The bartender came down the bar to see if Danny wanted a drink. He waved him away. "Come on, let's get out of here. I know another place."

The bartender raised his eyebrows, but didn't say anything in defense of his establishment. I think he took one look at Danny and was hoping we'd take our business elsewhere. I downed the rest of my beer and followed

Danny to the parking lot.

"I'm right here." He waved at a Bronco, black on black, some kind of lift kit underneath and tinted windows. "You wanna ride with me or you wanna follow?"

I've spent enough time with coke heads, speed dealers and the like to know that, no place to sleep that night or not, this could all go bad in as long as it took for the wrong synapse to fire. "I'll follow you," I said. He grabbed me in another bear hug that lasted just a little too long. His cologne hung in my nose, sweet, musky. I slipped out and went to the van.

Before I could back out, he swung around and gunned it; his taillights crested the rise a hundred yards away. I had to put my foot down to catch up, but the van wasn't made for speed. Visions of cops nestled behind billboards got the adrenaline going and I was a little less drunk, but my gut was churning. We wound through the new night, too quick past old landmarks gone, replaced by housing developments, a Dairy Queen, a strip mall that'd been around long enough to open and close in the time I'd been away, grass growing from the cracks in the parking lot. I did all I could to keep the two red beacons of his taillights in view. He had to slow down a couple times to let me catch up.

A few miles later, we cut onto a road I'd never traveled before. It took a while for me to realize it wasn't there when I was a kid. This was all woods back then, but now we sped past double-wide trailers and cookie-cutter beige box houses. After a mile or so, we crested another ridge and I saw neon in the distance.

Danny pulled off and I guided the van in beside him. He was blasting some hip-hop I'd never heard, plastic molding on his Bronco rattled so loud I could barely hear the music itself. He sat in the driver's seat, head bobbing, drumming on the steering wheel. He took an Altoids tin from a compartment in the dash and snorted a pinch of coke into each nostril. He powered the window down. "You want a toot? It's curiously strong." His eyes glistened in the neon. His teeth were bluish white. I raised a hand to signal "no thanks" and we headed inside.

No sign indicated the name of the place, nothing that said it was anything more than another low-slung cinderblock bar. The low rumble of some modern country, the lot around us filled with trucks, American cars. We were cradled in a little hollow. I tried to imagine what the place might have looked like before they cut the trees out and ran in the dusty gravel road.

"I own part of this place," he said as we pushed through the door into a small vestibule filled with two beefy hillbillies in black T-shirts and cheap khakis. They were frisking two other guys. The bouncers saw Danny and moved the paying customers to the side so we could go through.

I'd guessed before, but I knew for sure from the bouncers, that we weren't entering any old roadside bar. I'd seen guys like that many times before. I knew that inside would be a little desk where you could exchange big bills for singles, beyond that a bar, and in the center of the room, a raised runway with a pole placed at least on one end, if not both. If it was a fancier place, there might be a bullpen stage where girls went to warm up before the main stage, maybe a hot tub in the back, tubes of string lights looped around every surface, cigarette smoke, cheap perfume and talcum powder.

At the desk, Danny held up two fingers and the girl passed him two stacks of singles and he handed them to me: $40.

"Don't spend it all in one place," he said and winked. "Let's get a drink and then find yourself a seat and enjoy the show."

My eyes went to the stage. A blonde wandered through the lights, trying to swing hips she didn't have. Her eyes fell somewhere between the stage floor and the men in the seats that ringed the perimeter of the stage. She was in listless sync with the song—"Unskinny Bop" by Poison. Half a dozen guys ringed the stage in padded vinyl chairs. Some of them leaned forward, elbows on the edge of the runway, mooning up at the girl, while others leaned back, arms crossed, shrouded in the darkness just beyond the lights. The girl made her way to a man waving a fistful of dollars.

"You like?" Danny said. He handed me a shot glass filled with a thick brown liquid and nodded to the stage.

"She's skilled," I said.

"She's B league. You ain't seen nothing yet. I'll set you up with my girl."

I agreed with the first part of his assessment, but I wasn't sure how much I wanted to see. Did he mean his girl as in his child? Or did he mean his girlfriend? It was impossible to tell.

"You like Jaeger?" He downed his shot. I did not like Jaeger, but I also wasn't one to turn my nose up at free booze. The licorice-flavored syrup slid down my throat like a raw egg and stoked the fire that was already smoldering in my gut.

Danny put his arm around me and squeezed my neck between his forearm and bicep. "Man, it is good to see you.

I think about you all the time. We used to have some good times, didn't we?"

"That we did."

"You gotta tell me what you've been doing. I heard you were in New York."

"Yeah."

"You still making any music?"

"A little."

"You got a CD?"

"I recorded one. It hasn't come out yet."

"When's it coming out? I'll buy ten." He slapped me on the back again.

"I'll let you know." I thought about the useless master tapes in a box in the van. They officially belonged to the record label and that record would never see the light of day.

He waved for more shots. I was dizzy, too drunk.

"Leave the bottle," he said to the bartender. He turned to me. "You remember those times we had? Man, we had some times." He downed his shot and poured another. "Fucking Johnny Martin. Good to fucking see you, man. I always thought you were gonna be famous. I was sure I'd turn on the TV and you'd be on there. What happened?"

"It takes time. I'm working on it." I tried to smile.

"Whatever happened to that girl you were with in high school? You were in deep with her. Did you move to New York with her? What was her name? I can't fucking remember anything these days."

"Crystal," I said. "And no, we didn't end up doing that. I went alone."

He slapped me on the back again, this time so hard it made me cough. "It's fucking great to see you. I'm glad you called."

"Me too, brother." We toasted again. I looked across the room, pretending to be interested in the new girl, a brunette, taking the stage.

He said, "Hang out, man. I got some stuff to do in the back. I'll send you over a present."

I didn't want his present. I wanted to leave. I wanted to get gone. "That's all right," I said. "I just want to hang."

"Bullshit. You'll thank me later."

Danny drifted through the bar, very much the proprietor, squeezing shoulders, waving across the room, a thumbs up here, an Army salute there. Then he disappeared through a door by the stage.

I downed my shot and almost threw up. I willed my stomach to calm itself. The bartender took the shot glass away. "You want anything else?"

"I'll have a beer and you got anything to eat?"

"Doritos, pork rinds, that kind of thing."

"Give me some Doritos."

She pulled a bag off a rack hung behind the bar. "How do you know Danny?" she said.

"We went to high school together."

"Huh, that's cool." She looked across the room like she was searching for someone, but she just couldn't think of anything else to say.

"He a good boss?" I said.

"I've had worse."

After a pause of thirty seconds or so, the bartender deemed the conversation officially over and wandered down the bar to serve the two guys who were getting frisked when we came in. They were young guys, not much more than twenty-two or twenty-three. They were still wearing their work clothes, limestone-dusted Dickies from the quarry out near the Maryland border. Dad used to work there, too, for a while.

The brunette finished her two songs and hip-swung her way off the stage, collecting her clothes as she went and holding them to her chest like she was suddenly modest. Another girl, a redhead this time, teetered onstage wearing a white nurse's uniform and patent leather knee-high platform boots. She was busting out of the costume. She set herself, feet wide apart, back to the room, head down. Jackson Browne's "Doctor My Eyes" roared from the PA.

I sat through four dancers, feeling drunker all the time. I ate another bag of Doritos and waited for Danny to come back. I started thinking about the $40. It doubled the cash I had in my wallet and the bartender hadn't asked me to pay for a single drink. Mom came into my head. She was really gone. I should feel something. I finished my beer and ordered another. The bartender looked at me for a second, trying to decide if she should serve me, but she did.

A couple new dancers took the stage, a duo. They rolled around on the floor touching each other, miming fellatio. I almost didn't notice the girl slide onto the stool beside me. The song ended and the two girls collected their clothes and tip-toed off the stage.

"You John?" the girl beside me asked.

"I am."

"Dan told me to come over and keep you company."

She didn't sound too excited about her mission.

"That's OK," I said, "I'm just going to hang out."

I looked at her then. She wasn't dressed like the other girls; no costume or six-inch platforms, just a Police T-shirt, and a pair of cutoff jeans. She could have been dressed to wash her car. Her hair was somewhere between brown and gold and it caught the lights flashing off the mirror. Her eyes were green and there were tiny wrinkles around the edges of her mouth, not deep, but they framed her face. She had a lot of eye makeup on, so much that it made it hard to see what she really looked like. It was easy to tell she was very unhappy to be where she was.

"Dan told me to give you a dance," she said.

"I don't know," I said.

"Come on. If I don't, he'll think it was me that wouldn't do it, and then I'll have to hear about it. Just make my life easier."

"Let me buy you a drink."

She shrugged. It was the gesture of a young girl. I waved to the bartender.

"The usual," the woman beside me said. And she was a woman. I could see that now. She was at least in her late twenties, but maybe a little older. That made me wonder about her even more. Why was she here? The bartender poured her a Sprite and set it on the bar.

"Only the hard stuff for you," I said.

"I don't drink while I work."

"Never or anymore?" I was getting uncomfortable with how drunk I was. All at once, I wanted her to like me.

"Anymore."

"Fair enough," I said.

We were quiet. She sipped her Sprite.

"What's your name?" I said.

"Mist."

"No, I mean your real name."

"That is my real name."

"OK." I nodded. "It's like that."

"What?" She was suddenly angry. "In here, that's my

name."

"OK. Fine. Settle down."

"Just don't be a jerk."

We were quiet again. I was reminded of sitting in a movie theater on a date, junior high, wanting to reach out and hold the girl's hand but too paralyzed by possible rejection.

"Dan said you were 'his girl'," I said.

"Yeah, he would say that."

"It's not true?"

"We dated for a while, but months ago. Since then he likes to send me on these little missions to fuck with me."

"Like I said, I don't really want a dance. I can't afford it and I don't want you to do something against your will."

"It's paid for." She pulled a ticket out of her pocket, the kind that comes in a big roll that you buy as a chance in a church raffle. "And if I don't give you a dance I'll be in trouble. I need this job."

"You need it that bad?"

"This job makes good money compared to other stuff I could get. There's not a lot of employment choices around here."

"OK," I said. "You talked me into it. You're quite the salesperson."

She didn't respond to my joke. Instead she took another sip of her drink and led me to the opposite side of the room. Outside a curtained door was another beefy guy in the black shirt and khakis combo standing behind a podium, like a maître d'. On the podium, under a little black-light lamp, was a ledger, girls' names on the left and spaces across to list the number of dances they sold during the night.

"What'll it be?" the maître d' asked.

"Three songs," she said and handed the bouncer the ticket. He put it in a till under the podium. He put the number "1" beside her name. She looped her arm through mine.

"No touching," the bouncer said. "I can see you. Your hands come up from your sides and you're out...with prejudice." He was proud of the fifty-cent word. He hooked his thumb toward a closed circuit TV on a shelf to his right. It had a screen split in eights, in each frame a chair. There was no one in any of the rooms.

"No problemo," I said.

Mist led me through the curtain.

The private rooms were really just a line of booths separated by low walls and curtains suspended from the ceiling. She took me to the room farthest from the door. Inside was a high-backed upholstered chair, something you might find in an elderly aunt's sitting room, covered in form-fitting plastic. She took me by the shoulders and looked at me, head tilted down, eyes smoldering. As slack as her gaze had been before, it was keen now. My heart quickened a little. She pushed me into the chair and ran her hand across my chest as she moved to a shelf that held a boom box. She selected a CD from a stack by the box. When the music started, she swayed from side to side, hips fluid. The tune was low slung and industrial. I didn't recognize it, but I knew it from its influences: Big Black, Nine Inch Nails, Kraftwerk. The tune brought to my mind an assembly line of strippers grinding to the beat of the machines while they constructed bizarre implements of sex or death.

She came back to me as the vocals entered, a muffled,

whining moan. This, too, was a dance for her, one she'd done many times before.

"Just relax," she said and walked around me, touching me with her hands, her hair, her breasts, any part of her that could touch me as she moved. I was shocked at the transformation. I was a little afraid of her. She came full circle and faced me. "What do you like?" she said.

"I like you." And at that moment, I did, more than I expected to.

She arched her back and slithered her whole torso across my face. "What would you like me to do?"

"Anything you want."

She straddled me, pulled the T-shirt over her head, then unhooked her pink satin bra. She swayed to the music, grinding lightly, barely touching my jeans.

Strippers who are really good at their job have the gift of making the customer think the show they are putting on is real, just like any performer. But the stripper's performance is for one, not many, and it plays on the idea that at the end of the night, she might really want to go home with you, like the private dance is a courtship. I'd venture to guess that's where more than fifty percent of a stripper's money is made, from guys who chase the girl around after she's hooked him, buying drinks, depositing money in the garter when she takes the stage for her second dance of the night, or maybe even a second, longer private dance toward the end of the night into the next morning.

Mist removed the rest of her clothes. We moved into the second song. She climbed on my lap and ran her hair over my face. She blew in my ear and I shivered.

"Let's take this off," she said and peeled my jean jacket off my shoulders. She ran her fingernails lightly down the nape of my neck. My head was still spinning from the drinks and sadness was heavy on me.

She stepped back and danced in front of me through the final verse of the song and the coda. The last of the three songs came on. It was slower than the previous two, dirgeful. She walked to me, stepping to the beat. She looked into my face—not my eyes, but somewhere around my eyes. She turned away from me and sat on my lap, then threw her arms back and let herself pour off me to the floor. She climbed back up me, straddling me again. She started to grind hard as the pace of the song quickened. She arched her back and her breasts were near my mouth again, but I resisted the urge to bite them. They were so close.

She continued to rub herself against me and without warning I came in my jeans. I put my hands on her breasts and squeezed. She pushed off me and moved away. She looked sad and angry all at once. The bouncer slipped through the curtain as she slipped out. He grabbed my shirt with both hands.

I twisted out of the bouncer's grasp. The wet stickiness in my pants oozed. He swung at me. I ducked his right, but not completely. He caught me in the temple hard enough that I folded to one knee.

"Hey, I'm a friend of Dan's. It was an accident," I said.

His second blow hit me flush on top of the head. I went to the ground. I tried to grab at his feet and topple him over, but he saw me coming and stomped on my forearm. I lay prone and waited for the rain of blows, but it didn't come. He grabbed me by the collar and started dragging me out. Mist was gone like, well, mist. I wanted to see her one last time.

I expected Danny to come and save me at any

moment, but he didn't. The bouncer carried me by my collar and the waistband of my jeans, giving me a wedgie and squishing the mess in my pants around even more uncomfortably. Heads turned as I glided through the room. One of the two bouncers in the foyer held the exterior door open as my chauffeur pitched me into the night. I landed on the asphalt chest and face first. The pavement scraped a good burn into my cheek.

"I don't want to see you back here again," he said.

"I know Dan. He's my friend."

"I don't care if you know Jesus H. Fucking Christ." The door eased shut and the bouncers disappeared from view.

I lifted myself to sit Indian style on the pavement and touched my hand to the road rash on my cheek. My fingers came back smeared with blood. My face was on fire. I touched my ear and it throbbed. I could hear my heartbeat in it. Two guys came from the parking lot and stopped when they saw me sitting there.

"You all right, fella?" one of them said.

"Just had a little misunderstanding with the establishment."

"Broke the no-touchy rule, eh?"

 I nodded.

"You better get yourself on out of here. If you sit out here and they see you, they'll call the cops. Or they'll come out and give you a second helping. They don't like guys who break the no-touchy rule."

"I got that," I said and pointed to my face. The other guy held out his hand and helped me up. They both went into the club chuckling.

CHAPTER 3

When I hit the main road it came to me that I still had nowhere to go. I also didn't realize how drunk I was until I almost sideswiped a bank of mailboxes stationed at the entrance to a trailer park. I swerved. The tires squealed. I headed toward the opposite ditch. Somehow I got pointed down the road again. I eased off the gas a little. My face throbbed. I tried not to think about anything at all. I didn't even see the cop until I passed him doing at least 45 in a 25. He eased out behind me and hit the lights on his roof. He didn't turn on the siren. The lights were enough. The adrenaline started pumping. Fuck. I let the van drift to the shoulder.

The cop let me stew for a while. He sat in the cruiser and talked on his radio. Finally, he opened the door and walked toward the van with the heel of his right hand resting on the butt of his gun; in his other hand, a big flashlight. A car passed by slow. Two teenagers gawked at me sitting there waiting for the other shoe to drop as the cop approached the car. I fought the urge to flip them off. The taillights winked out beyond the next rise as the officer filled my window. He was a big man, wide and round. His belly cascaded over his belt, completely hiding the buckle. Dunlap's Disease my grandmother called it, as in, his stomach done lapped over his belt. I always laughed at that.

He twirled his finger to indicate I should roll down the window. He didn't bend down to speak.

"Do you know how fast you were going there?"

"No, sir," I said.

"I clocked you at forty-seven in a twenty-five."

"Oh."

He squatted down and shined the flashlight in my eyes. "Have you had anything to drink tonight, sir?"

"I did have a drink when I stopped for dinner a while back." I didn't want to outright lie—he could probably smell the booze—but I needed to minimize if I could.

"Step out of the car, please."

I couldn't get my hand around the door handle. The cop opened the door from the outside and I almost fell onto the pavement. He took me by the arm with his free hand and shined the flashlight into my face.

"How many drinks have you had, sir?"

"Two."

"What happened to your face?"

"I tripped."

"Please step to the other side of the vehicle."

He put me through the drunk tests. I failed them all. I couldn't walk a straight line. I couldn't lean my head back and touch my nose. I couldn't recite the alphabet backward.

"Please step to my vehicle," he said.

"What about my van?" I asked.

"I'm placing you under arrest for driving while intoxicated, sir. We'll have it towed to impound." He pulled my arms behind my back and cuffed me.

"All my stuff's in there."

"It'll be all right."

He led me to the back of the cruiser and we headed toward town. My stomach was on fire. I was light-headed and shaking.

"I'm going to get sick," I said.

"What?" He flung his right arm over the seat. "Speak up."

"I'm going to get sick."

He swerved the car fast to the shoulder, jumped out and pulled me by the shirt into the dust. I threw up what was left of the booze and Doritos into the dark silt of the shoulder. Bile dripped off my chin. I couldn't catch my breath.

"Mother of God," the cop said. He uncuffed one wrist and handed me a rough brown paper towel. I wiped my chin and spat into the dust. Some of the vomit had gone into my nose and the acid burned my nostrils.

"You about done or is there an encore coming?" The cop leaned against the rear fender of the cruiser and lit a cigarette.

"I can't tell yet."

"You some kind of junky or something?"

I shook my head.

"What the hell is wrong with kids today?" He wasn't talking to me.

"I'm thirty-one years old," I said.

"Going on ten." He recuffed my wrists and pushed me back in the car.

The cop turned off Route 7 just before we got to town and drove down what used to be an old access road behind the high school. This was the way to the old bus garage. It was also the route we took when we skipped out of school. The buses were the point of no return. If we made it to the yellow picket line of Bluebirds and got beyond them we knew we were free. Beyond was the Hamilton farm and the swimming pond and a day free of teachers, books, expectations.

When the cruiser rounded the corner and came on the old bus garage, I expected to see the same line of buses standing sentry in the lot, but there were no busses. In their place were a few police cars, a few trucks. The building was the same, but it had been repurposed.

"Why are we out here?"

"This is the police station," the cop said. "In case you haven't figured it out, we're not on a date here. I'm not taking you to the drive-in. You're spending the night in jail and in the morning we'll figure out what to do with you."

"No, I mean, this used to be the bus garage."

"Not for five years. The county sold the buses to a private service and moved the police out here. I didn't peg you from around here, with the out-of-state license and all." His tone was a little softer, but I still didn't get the feeling we were going to become friends any time soon.

"I grew up here. I moved after high school. I haven't been back in a while."

"Guess this is some homecoming." He laughed. "Martin. You related to the Martins used to have a place down on Green Lick?"

"Used to?"

"Yeah. You Ford Martin's boy?"

"Yeah."

The cop parked the cruiser in front of the garage. It was a half-moon of aluminum, with wide double doors large enough to accept a bus, but set into one of them was a small, person-sized door. The cop helped me out of the car and led me through the small door.

Inside, the place was cavernous. At the far end there were a couple police cars and an auto shop. Toward the front there were two trailers, the kind public schools set up as annex classrooms or construction sites use as offices. He guided me to the building on the left and we entered a wood-paneled office. Inside was a vinyl couch along one wall and three old Steelcase desks, worn and faded, initials scratched into the paint. Another cop, as skinny as my cop was fat, reclined against the far wall.

"Hey Devault, what'd you catch?"

"Speeding/DWI."

The other cop pursed his lips and nodded, impressed. "What'd you use?"

"Radar."

"Good choice, good choice." He dug a rub of snuff out of his lip and flung it into the trash can beside his desk. He took a sip from a Styrofoam coffee cup. "What's it like out there tonight?"

"Slow. Just this guy." Devault put me on the couch. "He says he's Ford Martin's boy."

"Is that right? Well, I guess it's true what they say about the apple and the tree." The skinny cop stood and stretched like a cat. "My turn to go catch me an evildoer. You enjoy your stay with us, Mr. Martin. We sure are glad you could stop by."

I wished I still had something in my stomach so I could puke on his shoes.

Devault had me blow the Breathalyzer, asked me a few questions, filled out some forms and then he led me across the way to the other trailer. It was exactly the same size as the office trailer, but instead of desks and a couch inside, this trailer had a row of iron bars screwed into the mottled brown shag carpet and the drop ceiling above. Another set of bars bisected the row of bars facing us making two cells, each with its own door, cot and toilet. In one corner was a kerosene heater. Devault flipped the switch on the heater.

"I can't stay in here," I said, "I'll suffocate."

"No you won't." He opened the door closest to us and guided me in. He shut the door. "Put your wrists against the bars." He uncuffed me and I sat down on the metal-framed bed. It squealed in protest at my weight.

"Sweet dreams, Mr. Martin." He flipped the switch on the wall as he left. Darkness. There were no windows in the trailer. The only light was the glow from the heater. I felt sick again and sat with my head between my knees until the nausea passed. I lay back on the bed. The pillow was old, case-less, flat and offered no support for my head. I folded it in half and lay there in the dark. It was already too hot in the room, but I shivered uncontrollably. My stomach ached. Blood pounded through my head. The hangover had already begun. I longed for a drink of water.

The last thing I remember thinking about was the trailer cell itself, how it should be called a Jailer. Lightheaded from the kerosene fumes. Would I die of carbon monoxide poisoning? My cheek ached. I wondered if Danny ever came back to look for me. Sleep came while I was considering whether or not I should call him in the morning to come and bail me out.

When I was really young, maybe four or five, I used to go out to the living room and sleep on the couch with Dad after he and Mom fought. There wasn't a time I could remember when they didn't fight and Dad would sleep on the couch when the battle died down. One of my first real memories was lying in bed, the light from the living room still on, Mom sucking hard on cigarette after cigarette, the *tank, tank, tank* of the ceramic ashtray banging on the glass-topped coffee table, the flick of the lighter as another cigarette flared. She waited for him and I waited with her, although I don't think she ever knew I was awake. Those nights waiting, sure that every sound outside was the approach of his truck, the anticipation of his slurred excuses or indignant denials of any wrongdoing, the yelling, Mom pounding down the hallway to their bedroom and then throwing his pillow into the living room. That act was the coda of the fight. I learned the tune well.

The nights he slept on the couch, I'd wait until I knew they both were asleep, pull my blanket from my bed and creep out. Dad slept on his side and the couch was too short for him, so there was a space behind his legs where I'd curl up and sleep until morning. Sleeping there, I felt closer to him than I ever felt again in my childhood. I had dreams sleeping there that I never had when I slept on my own, in my own bed. Most of them were good and I don't remember them, but one was recurring, the only recurring dream I remember having.

It started with a family picnic at a state park, the checked blanket on the ground, wicker basket, the whole deal. Mom and Dad happy and smiling at one another, touching each other, familiar, as they set out the food and Dad fired up the grill. The sun was out, but it was cool under the trees. Dapples of light played across the ground and I chased them like a kitten. We were happy.

But the way dreams do, everything changed all at once as we sat down to eat. The sun disappeared and the sky grew so dark it was almost impossible to see. In the real world you would expect rain, but in the dream the air stayed hot and dry. We continued to eat, but a groaning came from the trees. We all tried to ignore it at first, but it was no use. Mom was the first to look up. The trees had closed in around us. They formed a circle maybe ten feet around, moving in. Their trunks bent toward us and their branches reached. As quickly as we realized what was happening, one of the trees snatched Mom and she was gone. No screams, just gone. Dad scooped me up and ran for the car. Somehow we made it through the trees. He put me into the passenger seat and ran around to the driver's side. The trees were on us by then, tearing at him, the branches scraping like nails on a chalkboard against the paint. Somehow he was able to fight them off.

"What about Mom?" I said.

He didn't answer, fumbling with the keys. There was blood on his cheek, his forehead. The key slid into the ignition and the car came alive. He gunned the engine and yanked the gearshift into drive. The trees were all around us then, blocking the road. He slammed his foot to the floor and the tires squealed. I looked ahead of us and saw a slight opening. We could make it. We could get free. The sun was bright again beyond the circle of trees. We would be OK.

The trees lifted us off the ground. I looked over at Dad. He was so thin. Wasted. I could see the outline of his teeth through his lips. His skin was dry and he curled into the fetal position behind the wheel.

"Dad," I said. "What's happening?"

He turned to me as the trees shattered the glass and tore open the car like a can.

That's when I woke up, every single time, just before we were about to die. I had that dream maybe four or five times.

That night in jail I had the dream again. I woke sweating, out of breath, as scared as I had been all those years before.

I lay in the over-hot trailer sweating through my clothes. No idea what time it was. I listened for sounds that might give me some clue, but there was nothing: the muffled sound of two men talking, a car pulling into the garage. No one came into the trailer. My head was pounding, my mouth dry, my stomach caved in from hunger and nausea. My lips were cracked and swollen from too much mouth breathing while I slept. I turned over and the bile in my gut sloshed. My mouth began to water and I stumbled in the dark for the toilet. I puked up a thin, watery stream of nothing, stomach acid. It burned inside my nose. The smell of the puke filled the room, mingling with the heat. I thought I was going to die. I wanted to die. I slumped to the floor and let myself pool onto the carpet. It was cooler there. I fell back to sleep.

The rattling of keys in the exterior door brought me back. The stream of light from outside burned out my eyes.

"Jesus, Mary and Joseph." I recognized Devault's voice. I could see a fat silhouette. "I hope you're dead, because anything you could do to my jail to make it smell like this'll make me want to kill you myself."

I groaned a little and forced myself to sit Indian-style on the floor. My mouth was too dry to speak. Devault flipped the light on and the room flooded with fluorescent pale.

"Get up, princess. You've been sprung."

I managed to say, "What?"

"Bail. You know how this works."

"Yeah, but who?"

He put his hands into prayer position. "It always warms my heart when I can bring people together like this."

As he spoke, another man entered the room. I took

him in all at once: bone-thin, skin slack on his bearded face, white-haired, filthy red down parka, jeans three sizes too big, shiny on the thighs with dirt, grease. I looked at the jowly face, the pus-colored, sunken eyes. This man was obviously very sick. Devault had either dug this guy out of a grave or a Dumpster.

"Who's this guy?" I said.

Devault looked from me, to the man, back to me. He grinned. I turned back to the man and studied him a little more. I looked at his eyes behind the smeared lenses of the glasses dangling near the tip of his nose.

"Dad?" I said.

"John." His voice was still the same, a half-mumble.

"What happened to you?" I couldn't believe it was him. When I last saw him he was still a big man, beer gut and a shock of cow-licked brown hair. Now he was a wasted husk.

"I might ask the same thing." He stepped to the bars as Devault unlocked the cell. "You look like shit." We stared at each other for a half-minute, until I couldn't look at him anymore. I was ashamed I didn't recognize him, but he'd changed so much.

"Get yourself together," he said, "before I change my mind and leave you here where you can't do yourself any more harm."

There was no more talk while we went back into the office and Dad signed some forms. He opened his wallet and took out a check. Devault pointed to the amount he was to pay and he wrote it on the check. He wrote slow, careful. His writing was still the same pinched script I remembered. I couldn't stop looking at him. His uniform had always been western shirts unbuttoned, white T-shirt underneath, worn-out jeans and Dingo boots, but the man I followed was slump shouldered, lost in his clothes. He walked without lifting his feet from the ground. There was something in the way he moved that said that every motion caused him pain. He wore cheap-looking sneakers with wide Velcro straps. This couldn't be my dad.

Devault took us outside. It was cold and the sky was dirty white. The light brought the pain back into my head, a tiny hammer between my eyes. We followed Devault to a pickup at the end of the line of cars beside the building. He went around the driver's side and Dad went to the passenger's.

"Where are we going?" I said.

Dad yanked on the door and couldn't get it open. "To get your vehicle."

I opened the door for him. He couldn't raise his leg high enough to get in.

"You need some help?" I said.

"I can get it." He tried again. Devault did his best to pretend he wasn't paying attention.

"Let me help," I said. His shoulders drooped further and he nodded. I put my hands in his armpits. He wouldn't meet my eyes but I saw his face twist in pain as I lifted. He was light. Good God, he couldn't have weighed more than 150 pounds. I was scared.

Once he was inside he slid across the bench seat and I climbed in.

"Where's your truck?" I asked Dad.

"Don't have one."

"What happened?"

"Ask him." Dad nodded to Devault.

"Your Dad's a full-time pedestrian since we picked

him up last year. That got him his final letter in DWI BINGO. I personally took his license off him." Devault started the truck and backed out.

We drove down the access road in silence. Dad was never a big talker. When he did speak, his voice was a breathy rasp of permanent exasperation. As a kid, I always thought I'd disappointed him no matter what I'd done or didn't do. He was a private man, or at least he didn't say much. Even at that moment, we hadn't seen each other in years, him sick, me puking in a jail cell, the taste of it still in my mouth, the façade didn't break. He acted like he saw me yesterday, would see me again tomorrow and that the situation was nothing out of the ordinary.

As far as I could tell, he hadn't given me more than a quick once over. In my teen years, when he was gone and shortly before I left, I resented that he never opened up to me. Riding through town in Devault's pickup I understood his silence in a new way: by not saying anything during your weakest moments, it was possible to at least seem like you were strong.

The impound lot was out on the edge of the county. Devault left us in the truck while he went to retrieve the van. Dad and I didn't say anything for a long time.

"What the hell happened to you?" he said as we watched Devault and another guy walk into the car lot.

"I got caught drunk driving."

"That's not what I mean."

I didn't have an answer.

He continued, "You should have let somebody know where you were."

"What for? What happened to you?" My voice rose. I was angry and I hadn't expected that. The pain in my head cut me off.

"I don't want to talk about that." He looked out the driver's side window.

"That's too bad. You don't get to show up and I just forget everything because you bailed me out. I could have taken care of myself."

"Not from the looks of it."

Devault and the impound guy drove up in the van. I'd never seen anyone else driving it. It was a sad sight— champagne paint faded to rust, right quarter panel caved in, one headlight dangling, a desocketed eye, the windshield cracked horizontal port to starboard; my chariot.

"That's quite the vehicle you got there." Devault grinned as he handed me the keys. "Did it come with the roll of duct tape you use to hold it together, or did you have to buy that separate?"

"Go screw yourself," I said.

His face went dark. "There are about two dozen ways I can fuck you over for a good long time, son. That vehicle doesn't look like it would pass an inspection. Don't test me."

The rate at which he could change moods scared me a little. I'd known guys like him, who could be your best buddy one second and beat you half to death the next. Some of them were military guys I knew. The others were cops. It was best not to agitate them, so I stayed quiet and let them all have a good laugh.

I checked to make sure all my stuff was there. Dad leaned against the van, pale and breathing heavy.

"Young Mr. Martin, you remember that you have a date with the judge coming. It's in your best interests to stay in town until you get that worked out. We don't want to have to chase you down. And Ford, you remember you've got two weeks to vacate that land or I'll have to come and take you off it. You got your boy here. Maybe he can talk some sense into you."

Devault got in his truck and drove off. Dad and I stood looking at the ground.

"What was that all about?" I said.

"Nothing."

"Sounded like something. You don't want to tell me, that's fine. You tell me where to drop you and we can go our separate ways."

"You're my responsibility now, boy. I just bailed you out and you're not going anywhere."

"You write a check for the bail?"

He nodded.

"There any money in the bank to cover that check?"

"I'm meeting a guy later to sell him some tools."

"Jesus," I said. "I'm not staying with you."

"You don't have a lot of options."

"Where's your place now?"

"Up on the hill," he said.

"Devault said you didn't own that land anymore."

"We'll see about that."

"Well, you either do own it or you don't."

He didn't say anything.

"This thing's not going to make it up there," I said.

"You just have to get me a little ways down the road. I've got my truck stashed in the brush."

"I thought you lost your license?"

"You don't need a license to drive."

I made my way to the old family place like I'd been driving the road daily. I'd spent all those years riding with him after he picked me up from Mom's for a weekend. We turned off the main road right before the Kwik Stop came into view.

"Boulder still run the Kwik Stop?" I said.

Dad nodded.

"How's he doing?"

"One leg still shorter than the other." He laughed.

Boulder was born with one short leg and he wore a 6-inch rubber sole on his right shoe to compensate.

"You want to stop?" Dad said.

"No."

"If you're hungry we should stop. I don't have much up the hill. Not much of an appetite these days."

I turned and drove across the bridge. A hundred years ago, the Martins owned all this land, hill and valley. Now it sounded like Dad had let the last piece go.

"Is it cancer?" I said.

"Yeah."

"What kind?"

"Hell if I know. The kind that kills you. Doctor says it's everywhere. Started in the lungs. Probably got it from the asbestos at the power plant."

"You could sue." I have to admit that for a brief second I thought about the tapes, having the money to buy the record company out and release the record.

He waved the thought away. "What the hell for?"

"If the power plant's to blame, then they should pay."

"I looked into it. I signed something after the accident that said I couldn't sue if they gave me some money."

"How long do you have?"

"Doctor can't say. Or won't. Some days I feel all right. Not so bad today. Some days I can't move it hurts so bad."

I didn't know what to say. We drove into the valley.

My great grandfather built a house down in that valley back in the twenties. It started out as a one-room shack, but over time parts were added on. By the time I was born there were four bedrooms. It was a Frankenstein monster of a house with little wings branching off from every side. The last time I was there my grandmother was canning elderberry jam and the whole house smelled bitter sweet.

We approached the bowl of the valley, the bare winter trees gray as the sky and I saw the house, paint peeling, windows broken out, the old chicken coop fallen in on itself. Abandoned. Of course, she was dead, too.

"When did Grandmother die?" I said.

"Five years ago." He looked away from the house as we passed it. He was born there. It had to hurt him to see it like that. "Go around the back road," he said. "My truck's a little ways past the gas company gate."

If you didn't know it was there, you'd never see the access road to the back side of the family land, just a thin cut in the tree cover, two faint brown tire ruts in the undergrowth. I was afraid the van wouldn't even make it to Dad's truck, but it did. I got out and opened the gate, just as I had when I was a boy. The company bought the gas rights off Grandfather years before I was born and all over the property were little stands of orange-painted pipes that grew out of the ground like strange modern art exhibits. I never saw anyone from the gas company on the land in all the time I spent up there. I don't think anyone ever saw any money from what they took out, if they took out anything at all. I used to pretend the gas lines were parts of a great space ship buried underground and that's what made the hill so big. It was still imposing, the forest thick, the road barely visible, but it was smaller than I remembered.

"Park it on the other side of the gate," Dad said. I guided the van into the brush and Dad slid out slow. He made his way through the hip-deep thistle to a briar patch. He pushed the branches back to reveal a beat-to-hell Chevy pickup, cobalt blue dappled with putty red. He forced the door open and the truck started on the third try.

"Should I bring my stuff?" I said.

"I wouldn't leave it down here. Kids come back here to drink and fuck every now and then. Hard to say what might happen."

I got my duffle and threw it in the truck bed. I put the guitar in the cab.

"You ever learn to play 'Dueling Banjos'?" he asked. Years ago Dad promised he'd quit smoking if I learned to play that song.

"No." I said and helped him into the truck.

"Well, I guess it doesn't matter much now anyway." He laughed.

"You want me to drive?"

"I can drive." He swatted at me and I went to the passenger's side. He guided the truck through the trees, deep into the woods.

CHAPTER 4

One of the last weekends I spent with him on the hill, before he married Maggie and started to disappear from my life, I came to visit just after I turned twelve. We stood in the dining room of the cabin and he watched me tear the wrapping off the present he just brought into the room.

He said, "Happy birthday, John. Sorry your present's a little late."

The rifle was lighter than I thought it would be but still cold and solid in my hands. I ran my hand over the stock. The new wood was light and fresh, not dark from use like Dad's gun. My gun felt like plastic. The barrel was real though, cold and gritty-slick with gun oil. I worked the lever and the metal slid smooth, the hammer cocked, the empty chamber revealed itself and through the opening on top of the gun I could see inside the barrel. I wrapped my finger around the trigger but didn't pull it. I knew the gun wasn't loaded, but I was still afraid.

"I don't want you to tell your mother I gave you this gun," Dad said. "I'm going to keep it up here at the cabin and you can shoot it any time you're here, but if your mother ever finds out she'll call her lawyer and I might not get to see you again."

I held the gun in front of me and admired it. Dad gathered up the wrapping paper I threw on the floor and carried it to the wood stove. "Come on," he said, "you want to go out and shoot some cans?" He put a hand on my shoulder and smiled down at me.

I said, "OK," and swung the gun up and rested the stock on my shoulder like a soldier ready to march.

"Let me show you how to carry it," he said. "You always hold the barrel down like this."

He put the rifle in the crook of his elbow so the stock rested on his forearm just below the trigger guard.

"See," he said. "Now if you trip in the woods or something the barrel goes down and there's less chance you could hurt somebody."

He handed the rifle back and I placed it in my arm like he showed me.

"That's good," he said.

He picked some beer cans from the bed of the truck and walked into the field. A little ways out there was a hay bale and he set the cans up. He took a green and yellow box of shells out of his pocket.

He took six shells out of the box and slid them into the gun. He pushed each one in rhythmically, like he was hearing a song in his head while he did it.

He lifted the rifle to his shoulder, took a slow, deep breath and fired. My knees buckled. The middle can jumped into the air and fell behind the hay.

"Pretty loud, huh?" He handed me the gun. I tried to move like he moved. My heart beat fast and my arms shook.

Dad said, "It's gonna kick at you some and you have to hold it tight or your arm'll get bruised. Keep both eyes open and just look down the barrel. Try to get the front and back sights lined up at the can you're aiming at."

I couldn't focus on anything. I tried to let the rifle become a part of me, my arms, my eyes, but it was a cold, stiff limb that didn't respond.

"Now," Dad said, "take some air in, hold it, and when you're ready, squeeze the trigger slow."

I took a breath and held it. I tried again to line up

with a can but they floated beyond the barrel. I squeezed the trigger and fired without drawing a bead on anything. Next to my ear, the gun was louder than it was when Dad shot, like someone had hit me in the head with sound. All the cans remained on the hay bale.

"Good," Dad said. "That was good. You'll get one next time. How do you feel?"

"Deaf," I said.

He laughed. "You get used to that."

I faced the cans and fired, again and again. I reloaded, trying to find the same rhythm Dad had used as I pushed the bullets into the chamber. He stood back and watched. Sometimes he would encourage me. I started to get the feel for it. I started to understand how to focus my eyes on the cans and to line them up in the sights. After a few shots, I hit a can, then two, three. We went out and set them up again. I didn't hit one with every shot, but I was getting it.

Dad built the cabin himself, little by little, weekend after weekend when he still lived with us, and it never got completely finished. The downstairs had a living room with a cast iron wood stove, the couch from our basement and an old black and white TV. He'd had taken the appliances out of a camper and put them in the kitchen. A diviner found water and Dad sank a well and ran the water to the kitchen tap. He said that he had dug too deep and that was why the water always smelled like sulfur. It tasted OK though. The refrigerator didn't really keep things cold. There was a big chest freezer where Dad stored the meat from the deer he killed; deer steaks, deer burgers, deer sausages, hearts and livers and kidneys, wrapped in white butcher paper, dated and named with black magic marker, stacked neatly.

We slept upstairs in a loft that hung over the front

half of the ground floor. The open side of the loft looked down on the kitchen. The only way up was an aluminum ladder that Dad used to stand on when he cleaned the gutters. There was an outhouse out back that always stunk, no matter how much lime Dad dumped down the hole. The scent got into my nose and I smelled shit and ammonia for hours after.

I shot all the shells and handed him the rifle.

"Tomorrow," he said, "we're getting up early. Now that you have your own gun, it's time to get out in the woods and see if we can't get you a deer. What do you think about that?"

I thought of walking through the woods carrying my gun, shooting at things. It was exciting, but it scared me, too. He was waiting for an answer.

"OK," I said, afraid to hurt his feelings or make him mad by saying anything else.

"You feel like going into town?" he asked. "I wanna buy you a Coke."

"I guess," I said.

Going to town meant going to the VFW or the Dipsie Doodle. Going to town was better than staying in the cabin, trying to get a TV station on the rabbit ears and watching him get mean. He scared me at night. After the sun went down and there was no more work to do he was restless. He got a look in his eyes like he was waiting for someone and they hadn't shown up.

"Let's hit the road," he said.

Hank Williams was on the VFW jukebox. Cigarette smoke hung low and stung my eyes. I held my breath until I felt ready for the smell of the place: tobacco, vomit, ammonia. Along the bar there were stations of saltshakers and small cans of V8.

Dad nodded to some of the guys at the bar. Jimmy Calhoun was at the end of the bar, one elbow leaning on the rail.

"Looky at these two men around town," he said. "You fellas out lookin' for trouble?" Jimmy was already pretty drunk. It was easy to tell. He stood with his hips thrust out, his thumb through a belt loop, a cigarette between his index and middle fingers. The cigarette had burned down to the filter and wasn't lit any more. He waved to the bartender and she went to work getting us drinks. "First round's on me, gents." He slapped Dad on the shoulder and Dad gave him a look, like he didn't want to be touched. I hoped Jimmy noticed, because I didn't like to be around Dad when he gave people looks like that. Jimmy was the only friend of Dad's I knew. I liked him, even though he was always a little out of control. I liked that he smiled, he had fun. When he was around it was like nothing could go too bad.

Jimmy pulled out a stool for Dad, near the jukebox and the pool table. The jukebox had little tubes that, at one time, bubbled with colored water but they were all broken and empty now. Only one of the speakers worked. The bartender was an old lady with thinning hair the color of damp cigarette ash. She placed a beer in front of Dad and a fountain Coke in front of me without saying a word.

Dad dug a handful of change out of his jeans and put it in front of me. "Go ahead back there and play a little pool."

The pool table only had three legs. Two cinderblocks had replaced the broken leg and they weren't quite as tall as the rest of the table, so no matter how true your shot it always leaned to the cinderblock side. I put two quarters in and listened as the balls rumbled through the ramps and banged into the hopper at the rack end. I bounced them off the rails and let them stop wherever and then I just shot at them, trying for trick shots and combinations. When all the balls were down I put another two quarters in and did it again.

A tall man with long, stringy, slicked-back hair, walked to the jukebox, slotted in money and punched numbers. He played "Luckenbach, Texas" and sang along loud as the first lines came. He swayed from side to side out of time with the music. As the song reached the second verse he pushed his voice harder, more off-key and rough.

Dad said, "Why don't you shut the hell up, Bill?"

Bill stopped singing. "Why don't you make me, Ford?"

Dad motioned to the bartender with his empty beer bottle.

"This ain't high school anymore, Ford," Bill said. "You ain't the guy anymore. You're just like the rest of us. If I wanna come in here and put money in the jukebox and sing along to the song I paid for then I will."

The bartender looked at Dad with an expression like she had seen this before and wanted none of it. She looked at Jimmy, but he was leaning back on the bar, watching.

Bill pushed off the jukebox and leaned on the corner of the pool table. "You think you're so fucking good? You come in here and sit by yourself and don't say nothing to nobody, like you own the place. Well, I got news for you buddy: you ain't no better than any of us. You're a fuckin' piece of shit." Bill turned back to the jukebox.

Dad said, "You're a big man to tell a guy off like that. Why don't you come on over here so we can keep talking?"

"I'm done saying what I had to say."

"I don't think you are done."

"At least when I come out to get drunk I leave my kids at home," Bill said.

Dad slid off the stool and took three steps to the jukebox. He grabbed Bill by the hair and smashed his face into the cracked plastic window. The jukebox skipped twice then stopped playing altogether. Dad let go of Bill's hair and he fell to his knees. He reached out to grab the pool table. I moved back against the wall, my heart beating fast. I wanted to run away. I wanted to kick Bill in the face.

Dad slapped his hand away from the pool table and punched him in the ear. He fell to the floor and coughed blood across the linoleum. Dad stood over him and drew a breath like he wanted to say something, but instead his arms fell to his sides. He stepped back and looked at me still pressed against the wall. Our eyes met for a second and then he got a look on his face that was both angry and filled with shame. He wedged his boot under Bill's hipbone and swept him against the jukebox. Jimmy stumbled over and grabbed Dad in a bear hug. Dad shrugged him off. Jimmy lost his balance and fell to the floor.

Dad clenched his fists. "Stay the fuck off me," he said.

"Jesus, Ford. What the hell's wrong with you?"

Dad looked at Jimmy and I was afraid he was going to start hitting him. I moved to his side and he saw me again.

"John," he said, "come get in the truck." The bartender stood at the end of the bar holding half a broken pool cue, ready for whatever came next. She watched us leave. I walked close behind him, trying to match his gait, fighting the urge to run out ahead of him.

He started the truck and pounded on the steering wheel. He ran his hands over his face.

"Don't ever do that," he said. His knuckles were bleeding and he wiped them on his jeans. There were dark hairs from Bill's head laced between his fingers. "No matter what, don't ever do that."

He gunned the truck through town, going too fast and I was scared. He didn't slow for any curve. We reached the road that took us back up the hill. He took it fast and I held onto the armrest to keep from sliding around.

"Dad, slow down," I said.

He looked at me, angry. I braced for him to hit me.

"Sorry," he said. When we emerged in the field he drove past the cabin to the highest ridge and killed the engine. It was quiet. The light from the fingernail moon just above the trees lit the cab of the truck. Clouds like smoke wafted between us and the blue-black sky.

"Look over there." He pointed into the darkness at the tree line. "You see him?"

"I don't see anything," I said.

"He came out from between those two big trees. He's a big one, ten point at least."

The tree line was nothing more than a darker patch of dark.

"I can't see it," I said.

"Keep your eyes out there and let them adjust, see if you can see him move."

A cloud went over the moon and there was no light at all. We sat there for a long time and neither of us spoke. I listened to Dad breathing.

"He's gone," he said after a while and started the truck again.

At the cabin, I peed into the weeds beside the porch. I was too scared to go all the way to the outhouse in the dark.

Dad didn't wait for me. I followed him inside when I was done. I held my hands over the wood stove but it was cold. I didn't know how to relight it. I climbed the ladder to the loft. Dad was a dark shape in his cot.

I said, "Good night, Dad," softly and he didn't reply. I padded blind through the black room and crawled into bed wearing my coat and all my clothes. I tucked the wool Army blanket tight around me but tried to keep its coarseness off my skin. Wind knocked the electric lines against the tar paper outside. I don't know how long I lay there, not sleeping, listening to the sounds of the woods, a train in the valley below. Nothing made sense to my twelve-year-old mind. I watched his form on the cot, the rise and fall of his breathing in the moonlight.

I woke to the smell of eggs and bacon cooking. The cabin was warm. Dark morning light grew behind the trees outside the window.

I went down the ladder as Dad scraped the food onto plates. He carried them to the table.

"Come sit," he said. He drew in a breath like he was about to speak, but stopped. He moved his fork around in his eggs and said, "I want to apologize for what I did last night. That was no way for a man to act and I wish you wouldn't have never seen that."

"It's OK, Dad," I said.

He lifted eggs to his mouth and chewed them slow. He was looking past me, out the window to the field and the woods. "You ready to get out in the woods?" he asked.

I tried to see the gun in my hands among the trees and a nameless anxiety rose in me. "I don't know," I said.

"Do you not want to go?" He didn't look at me, trying to be soft.

"It's not that. I mean, I don't know if I want to kill something." I stared down at the table. "I'm scared," I said.

Dad reached across the table and put his hand on top of mine. He squeezed my fingers hard. He said, "I felt the same way when my Dad took me out the first time. I didn't want to. You won't know until the time comes if you can pull the trigger. And after that you'll know. It won't mean you're better or worse, it'll just mean you know."

We ate the rest of our breakfast in silence and I watched the sky turn pale blue out the window, almost no color at all, a winter sky.

"We gotta get out in the woods before it gets too late," he said.

He went into the living room and came back with our guns. He watched me load and check mine. When I was done he said, "Good. That was good." We put on our coats and boots and walked out into the field.

"You take the lead," he said. "Let's see if we can't pick up that big fella we saw last night. I'll spread out to the right, that way we'll both have a clear shot on all sides. There's a way to see deer in the woods; you look and you don't look. If you let your eyes take everything in, that's when you'll see. If we see him, the first shot is yours."

We walked through pools of fog to the far tree line and entered the woods, fighting through briar patches and walls of rhododendron until the undergrowth got thinner. I tried to imagine myself as part of the woods. I became anything I touched. I made no sound.

We walked slow, angling down the hill for a half hour before we stopped. Dad bent down and moved some leaves with a stick. He looked at the track he had found and then pointed further down the hill.

We walked along a creek that ran through the valley floor. My feet got so cold they hurt and then they stopped hurting. I should have worn a second pair of socks. We rounded a bend in the creek and found a thicket of orange gas lines. Dad slung his rifle down and rested the butt on the ground. I leaned back on a tree trunk and tried to move my toes. Silence rushed in around us like a waterless flood.

Movement in the brush.

I scanned the trees, looking and not looking: a big buck. Dad saw it too but didn't pick up his gun. He was waiting for me. I raised the rifle to my shoulder and pulled it tight. I sighted down the barrel, kept both eyes open and drew in a deep, slow breath. The deer came into focus in the sights, the morning sun creating a halo of light all around it. The buck floated off the ground, rising first above the low-lying brush then into the tree limbs above. I followed it with the rifle barrel. My knees shook and I couldn't hold the gun still. The deer looked at me, glowing in the light, floating there above the forest floor, and I squeezed the trigger slow. The sound of the shot ricocheted against the hills.

The deer was gone. Dad ran up the hill and I ran after him.

"Goddamn it," he said as he reached the place where the deer had been. He was panting from the run. He felt around on the ground and his hand came away covered lightly in blood.

"You got him," he said.

We followed the blood trail through the bramble for a few hundred yards until we found the deer lying on its side breathing quick and shallow. Blood burbled from a wound just below its shoulder.

"You got him, boy," he said. "That was one hell of a

shot. You got him good. Should be some good meat there."

The deer continued to breathe hard and quick and its black, shining eye rolled around wild and scared. Dad took out his hunting knife and handed it to me. He held the deer's head with one hand and guided the blade to its throat, his hand around mine.

Together we drew the blade into the fur, then skin, muscle, cartilage. Air burst out of the new wound and the deer's head tilted farther back. Blood spit from the wound and soaked into the leaf bed.

Dad looked me in the eye. His gaze was cold and blue. He guided my hand again and notched the knife into the deer's belly and ran it down the length of the deer's stomach fast, and the deer's insides spilled onto the brown leaves. He reached into his pocket for a big plastic bag and cut several organs free, placing each one in the bag. He said, "Liver, heart, kidneys—the rest we'll leave for the foxes."

Steam rose off the organs. Dad's hands and arms were covered with blood. The air around us smelled like iron and sweat.

"You take this," he said and held out the bag. The deer parts pressed up against the plastic and I thought, *Fish in red water*. I slid the gun into the crook of my arm and took the bag.

"You did good," he said. "I'm proud of you. I really am."

He took up the hind legs and started up the hill. I followed carrying the bag of organs. They warmed my hands. I was excited by the heat of them. The deer's antlers caught on a root and Dad stopped to free them, gently twisting the head back and forth. I moved around him and kept walking. I couldn't look at the deer; its black dead eye, its empty, open belly. I saw the crest of the hill above us and I wanted to get there.

CHAPTER 5

I could still feel the way the deer parts slipped through my fingers as I held that bag. I was in the memory as we crested the hill, so I didn't see the destruction all around me at first. The road was almost gone, falling over the hill in places, washed out. The truck crawled slow over sections that were so narrow that from the passenger's side window I couldn't see road, only the chasm below. I looked over at Dad, and I was frightened by what I saw. He was a pale sweat of concentration. I wanted to tell him to stop and let me drive, but there was no way to get out of the truck on the thin strand of handmade road. I didn't want to distract him either. We continued on, closer and closer to the top and I mouthed a prayer over and over.

I could see the crest of the hill through the leafless winter trees. I scanned the field. My eyes crossed the space where the cabin should have been, but it wasn't there. We came closer and I could see the cinderblock foundation, electrical wires hanging from the pole that was just outside the window where I used to sleep. The structure itself was gone.

"Where's the cabin?" I said.

"Gone."

"I can see that."

"It burned down."

"How?"

"They say electrical, but I say not."

"What do you mean?"

We came out of the woods and he stopped the truck. I stared into the hole where the cabin used to be, overgrown, the appliances, charred and warped, lay among the blackened two by sixes. A patch of shingled roof. The seat from a riding lawnmower. A screen door with no screen. Garbage bags, some broken open and some still intact.

"You remember Maggie?" he said.

Maggie was the woman he married after the divorce was final, the woman he'd been sleeping with before he moved out. She came to live with him the summer following that day we went deer hunting. I heard they got divorced sometime while I was still in high school and I was glad. I hadn't thought about her in a long time and I didn't want to now.

"I remember her," I said.

He went on to tell me about how they got remarried after Grandmother died and she moved in with him again. I never understood his attraction to Maggie. She was tall—almost as tall as him—and thick. Her arms seemed too long for the rest of her, her hips too wide, her ass flat, her hair cut short in a way that couldn't be effectively styled. There used to be a picture of them on their wedding day hanging in the cabin. Her in a calico dress and Dad in a powder blue tux and his best Dingos. Someone had tried to do her hair up nice, but it looked like a wig that had been given a haircut by an eight year old. I wasn't invited to the ceremony, or at least I thought I wasn't, and it was another item on the long list of hurts. It occurred to me as I listened to him spin out the tale of their remarriage, that I could have very well been invited, but hadn't been told. I wanted to give him that credit, even though he hadn't earned it.

"You know," he said, his voice quiet, only breath, "sometimes a person gets into you like an infection. I knew a boy when I was a kid who got caught on a barbwire fence and got rust in his blood and died. Tetanus. That's how I felt with her. She got in me and I couldn't get her out." He was breathing hard, worn out from talking. He stopped for a minute and then continued. "I always felt bad. You had it tough. She was a hard woman and jealous of you. I should have told you that. I always wanted to. The words were in my head, but I couldn't put them together. When you're young, you don't know there's different kinds of love.

"We split up and I went off to the Eastern Shore. Worked there for a long time. Carpentry, whatever I could get. Had a little trailer. I was nothing. I was lonely. I couldn't stop thinking about her. I drank a lot then, two, three years like I was on fire, but eventually one day I found myself on the road and back here again. I wanted to get out of here. Too many bad things happened, but this place was in me too, like the iron in that boy. I don't know what it is about a place, but everywhere else I went I kept looking for something familiar. I wanted everywhere to feel like here and it never did. I had to come back. Took me a couple years to work up to seeing Maggie again and then we were together like it was before. When Mother died she left me some money and me and her fixed up the cabin, made it a house."

"Did you finally cover the tar paper with siding?"

He laughed. I'd forgotten his laugh. It was like a smoker's cough with a little "hee-hee" at the end.

"We did. You wouldn'ta recognized the old tar paper shack. It was tan, like the siding on the old house. I always liked that color."

He didn't say anything more for a long time, but I knew that wasn't the whole story. There were beads of sweat on his brow and I wondered how bad the cancer really was, but I knew I'd never get a straight answer out of him. He cut the engine and it was quiet. The motor ticked softly as it cooled. I'd forgotten how silent it could be up there.

He said, "I don't know if you knew she had a son from her first marriage. He was older. She had him when she was eighteen. He went to live with his father before I knew her. Down in Georgia. Well, he got in some trouble, crack cocaine and the police and all that, and he got put in jail. She went down there and got him and brought him up here. That's when the trouble started. He and I didn't get along. Wasn't more than a week before the fights started. He was a mess and mean as hell from coming off the drugs. All skin and bones and meanness, like an old cat. One Sunday me and him had a big fight. Maggie always took his side and so I went out to the shed to cool down. I was out there a couple hours and drank a few beers and then I heard these dogs that'd been running deer howling back in the upper field." He waved toward the place where he saw the buck in the dark that night. "I got my 30/30 and went out to track them. Maggie's boy seen me with the gun and called the police, had me arrested—assault with a deadly weapon and some other shit. I did ninety days in jail and by the time I got out she and that boy were gone. She'd sold the house and the land. I had to put it all in her name on account of my debts. If your mother knew I had money she'd have come after me."

"You did owe her child support, like ten years' worth."

"You were long out of the house by then. It was my money from Mother."

A hawk flew over the field and circled. It caught an air current and floated for a long time, around and around.

"You know where Maggie went?" I said.

"I thought she might go down to Morgantown, stay with her folks, but she wasn't there. The boy neither. I think they might have gone back to Georgia."

"What happened to the cabin?"

"That's what it looked like when I came up here after I got out of jail. The fire marshal said it was electrical, but I don't believe that. I run that wire myself. I know it was good." He said "wire" and it sounded like "war." I'd forgotten that part of his accent. Same with "fire." It came out "far."

"And that's it. You let her go with all your money?"

"By then I knew I was sick. It doesn't matter."

Silence again. I looked out over the field, much the same as it had been when I was a boy. Knee-high grass deep enough to hide in, wild strawberry bushes and Queen Anne's Lace. How many times had I been there? Two dozen? Less? But it seemed like I spent my whole childhood on this hill. The memory of it outweighed the rest of my life. I can't say why.

"Where have you been staying if there's no cabin?"

He hooked his thumb in the opposite direction of the gaping foundation, toward the tree line. I hadn't seen the camper when we first pulled up, all my attention went to the ruined cabin.

The camper might have been a sorrier sight still. A squat little pull-behind camper, the trailer hitch supported by two scorched cinderblocks taken from the cabin foundation. The camper had been aluminum sided at the beginning of its life, but along the way patches of the siding had fallen off. The tiny screen door on the back was pitted and warped, screens ripped out of the tiny side window.

He started the truck and drove the thirty yards to the camper dooryard. We sat in the truck for several seconds. I was waiting for him to get out. He didn't move.

"I can't get out," he said. "I need help."

I came around to the driver's side and lifted him to the ground. Again he didn't meet my eyes as I held him.

"Do you need me to carry you?"

"Fuck no. I just can't get my legs to work up and down like that. Hurts like a mother."

"You sure?"

"Just put me down." His face screwed up with pain as he took his weight on.

"Maybe you should go to the hospital."

"Mind your own goddamn business." He tried to smile at me, pretend he wasn't angry, but I heard the old edge in his voice.

Inside, the camper was ripe. The little sink was piled high with food-crusted plates. Half-empty cans of chili furred with mold. Every surface was covered with trash.

"Jesus," I said.

"It's the maid's week off."

"How long have you been living in this thing?"

"End of summer."

"How have you survived? You're not working, are you?"

He shook his head. "I get disability. My back was never right after the power plant accident either. I finally got the government to pay me some for it. I get a hundred fifty a month."

It occurred to me that the camper had no bathroom. "Where do you go to the toilet?" I said.

He threw his arms wide to indicate wherever. He said, "Outhouse probably still works if you want privacy."

I could see it through the small window over the

sink, a tiny shed with a corrugated fiberglass roof to let the sunlight through. The fiberglass had once been green, but had faded to a skin tone over the years. The thicket was heavy all around it. It didn't look like anyone had used it in a long, long time.

"Not exactly a beaten path in that direction," I said.

"I haven't been able to walk that far in a while. If I have to go I use a pot and throw it in the woods when I feel good enough."

We sat for a long time saying nothing.

"What do you do for food?"

"Boulder brings me a box of stuff every couple weeks."

The sun slipped behind the trees. Soon enough it was cold in there.

"Must get cold up here."

"Just recently. I got a kerosene burner, but I like it cold. And I got several of your grandmother's quilts. It won't be fun, but we'll survive."

I looked out the window at the setting sun burning through the trees. Soon it would be dark and that would be it. No light, just dark.

"You got anything to drink?"

"A couple jugs of water. No booze. I can't take it anymore. Doesn't sound like it sets too well with you either."

"You've got a point."

We were quiet again. After the city, jail, the road, the quiet made me nervous. The trash in the place closed in on me. I couldn't draw a breath, a panic attack coming on. I tried to breathe slow to keep the anxiety down, but it crawled up my back, through my shoulders and all the things I didn't want to think about came to me. Dad curled up on the couch that turned into a bed and lay looking at me. I turned away from him, but I knew he was watching. I worried about what he thought of me, even though I knew it didn't matter.

"It's good to see you again, John," he said.

I didn't answer. I heard him take a breath like he was going to talk again, but he didn't.

"When was the last time you saw Mom?" I said.

"Four, five years ago. Ran into her in town. Funny that didn't happen more than it did. We talked for a minute. I asked if she heard from you. She said no."

"Did you know she died?"

"I did. I thought about going to the funeral, but that was right when Maggie and I got back together."

A barn owl in the trees somewhere behind the camper called out.

I said, "I didn't even know she died. I hadn't talked to her in years."

He didn't say anything for a long time. I listened to the owl.

Dad said, "That's something you'll have to live with."

A little while later he was snoring. The moon rose—a half moon. The sky was clear and it cast a silver light over the dead tall grass of the field. I wanted to curl up and sleep. I wanted to run. I was shaking all over from wanting a drink. I didn't know what was coming next, but I knew I had to meet it.

When the moon was halfway to its apex, I cleared off the overhead bunk and crawled up, careful not to wake Dad. In the moonlight, he looked wasted away, dead already. I put my hand in front of his nose to make sure he was still breathing. On the bunk, I covered myself with two quilts. It was so cold I kept my shoes on. I lay there shivering, thinking sleep was not going to come. The owl had stopped talking to me. Dad's breathing changed. His chest began to rattle. Sleep came eventually.

I was up early the next morning. I watched the sun light the window. Quiet. The wind rustled the trees. Bird calls. Dad was still asleep.

I started cleaning up the camper. There was barely enough room in the thing for one person when there wasn't a ton of junk piled everywhere, but as it was I had to wade through knee-deep garbage just to get from one end to the other. I filled bag after bag and dropped them outside the door. Eventually, the floor emerged, the countertops and table. Dad woke up and lay on the bed watching me. He was paler than the day before.

"You feeling OK?" I said.

"I've been better. A lot of pain." His voice was barely a whisper. I got scared again. I didn't know how to take care of a dying man.

"You should let me take you to the doctor."

"There's no reason to go to the doctor. He can't do anything."

"What about some pills? I could go get them. At least then you'd feel better."

"I don't want it." He turned his face to the wall and that was the end of the discussion.

I filled five more garbage bags. When the place was clean, I took the bags and threw them in the cabin foundation. I stood on the crest of the hill and looked over the field. It was cold. The sky was white, the corona of the sun just barely visible, a halo of white, through the haze. What month was it? What day of the week? It seemed like years since I last knew the day. When the band was gigging,

I was tied to the calendar, always looking for the next gig, setting up the tour, worried if this or that A&R guy was coming to the big show, if we'd make enough over the door to get asked back again. I was always worried.

Back inside the camper, Dad was asleep again or pretending to keep me from talking to him. Anxiety welled up in me. The sun was barely above the trees and I could think of nothing to do. I looked in the cupboards. Nothing but two more cans of chili and a tin of SPAM. The last of the water jugs was almost empty. I was hungry. I stood at the window and looked at the truck parked a few yards away. I was afraid of it. I was afraid of everything. It washed over me in that moment that I'd lived my whole life afraid. I didn't want to be afraid anymore. I went out and got in the truck.

I parked where we'd uncovered it the day before and tried to hide it. I didn't do a good job of camouflaging. It looked like a truck with branches on the windshield. I took a few steps back and it looked better. It seemed childish to be hiding a truck in the woods. I got in the van and drove to town.

I told myself I was going for supplies. I still had Dan's forty bucks in my wallet. I could get enough to hold us over. I could buy a coat and some more practical clothes for the environment. But I knew I was going to town for something else. I could feel it as soon as I hit blacktop. I fought it all the way through the hollow past Grandmother's house. When I came out of the valley my mouth was watering for the first drink but I forced myself to go to the Nearly New shop and browse the clothes.

In the days leading up to the seventh grade I was faced

with a crisis I didn't know how to solve. I knew we were struggling for money. Mom had a job as a secretary, but it didn't pay much. We ate a lot SPAM casserole those days. That fall I started junior high. It was in the same school building as the elementary where I'd gone for six years, but in a different section of the school, the newer section. There were individual classes and the kids got to walk through the halls in between. I'd seen them holding hands, kissing, laughing. It was like a different world, a more grown-up world, and I wanted to fit in. This was the early eighties and that year Izod shirts were the rage. Most of my clothes were bought at the Nearly New Shop and smelled of mothballs. I had no idea where you could even buy an Izod. One afternoon I was downtown with Mom. We were going to the library to return some books. Across the street I saw a boy wearing one—pink, collar popped—he looked awesome. I pointed him out to Mom.

"I want a shirt like that," I said.

"Really? I didn't know you liked pink."

"Not pink, but that kind of shirt. Everyone's wearing them."

"Where do they sell them?"

"I don't know, maybe at the mall in Morgantown."

We both watched the boy cross the street and turn the corner. I didn't know him. He was an older boy. I wanted that swagger and I was sure that the Izod would give it to me.

The next weekend we drove to Morgantown. I loved to go to the mall. They had a record store there. I bought my first record there when I was eight (Kiss—*Alive II*) and I still saved all of my allowance money to buy records whenever we went. At that time, I was working my way through the

Beatles catalog. By the time I was out of high school I could sing every part of every Beatles song. For a long time they were my religion. It started not long after I bought the KISS record. A TV station out of Pittsburgh started showing the old Beatles cartoons in the half-hour slot right after I got home from school. Mom was still at work, I was all alone and John, Paul, George and Ringo were my babysitters, my best friends. The music was like nothing I'd ever heard before, both raw and alive, but precise too. It was the harmonies that got me. And never let go.

I got a dollar a week when I was eleven and we hadn't been to the mall in a couple months so I thought I had enough for two records. We got to the mall and finally found the Izods in the most expensive store in the place. They were $35. I knew as soon as I saw Mom's face that there was no way we could afford one.

"I'm sorry, Johnny," she said. "That's just too much. If your goddamn father would pay his child support we could do it. You're still growing. You'll grow out of it before you wear it enough."

I didn't want her to go off on another rant about Dad and his non-payment of child support. She was angry a lot then, usually about money. I knew that something like this was enough to send her into a quiet night of seething on the couch, the cherry of cigarette after cigarette lighting her face in the dark.

"It's OK. I don't like any of them anyway."

"What color do you like?"

I looked at the rack and picked out a color I didn't see. "Orange."

That seemed to make her feel better.

"Do you want to go to the record store?" she said.

I stared at the shirts on the racks, the huge number on the price tag. How could anyone spend that much on a shirt? I thought about the ten dollars in my pocket and was embarrassed by how small the sum was.

"No. I'll wait until next time."

I didn't think too much about the shirts again for a while. When I saw a kid in school wearing one there was a brief pang of envy, but I accepted my lot. I was not meant to have an Izod and that was that.

A month later, I came home from school one Friday afternoon and Mom was bouncing around the house excited. There were times in those years when she darted around the house, cooking, cleaning, singing along to the radio. She'd only just started dating Stan and she seemed happy. It was a nice warm Friday afternoon and I decided to go with it, to let myself be happy with her. Friday was pizza day and I loved pizza more than anything. I went to my room to read and listen to music while she finished cleaning and then we went downtown to pick up a pizza. You wouldn't think it, but there's some pretty good Italian food in West Virginia. A lot of Italians came to the hills to work in the mines and stayed. Our favorite pizza place was called Scotto's. It was owned by two brothers who came from Brooklyn with their families when they were kids and opened a pizza place when they got out of high school. I didn't realize how good the pizza was in my hometown until I went to New York and tasted New York pizza. Scotto's was not too far off.

After dinner Mom started getting fidgety again and I knew she had something to tell me. I was afraid to know what it was.

"What's going on, Mom? You seem way happy."

"I have a surprise for you," she said.

"What?"

"In my room."

She bounced out of her chair and I followed. I couldn't help but feel some of her excitement.

On her bedspread I saw the familiar plastic bag of the Nearly New Shop, or more specifically, a plastic bag bearing the name of another long-dead store. The Nearly New didn't have bags of their own. They bought the bags of other stores that had gone out of business. Mom sat down on the bed beside the bag.

"Go on and open it," she said.

I folded back the mouth of the bag to reveal some peach-colored fabric, decidedly feminine. I recognized the weave of the fabric. It was an Izod.

"Wow," I said. "I can't believe you found an Izod at the Nearly New."

"I couldn't believe it either. I was in there because someone at work told me they had some new control top panty hose on sale and I walked past the boys' clothes and there it was."

I lifted the shirt out of the bag. I was excited to try it on. I unfolded it to get a look at the long-desired alligator. My stomach fell. There on the breast was not the alligator, but instead the running fox of the JC Penney Izod knock off. Kids who wore those in school were laughed at behind their backs. I heard some of the rich kids call one boy, who I knew lived right in town, a piker. There was no worse name to be called than piker. Even the kids who lived on the pike beat the hell out of anyone who called them piker when they heard about it. Mom must have seen the disappointment in my face.

"What's wrong? Is it the color? I didn't know if you'd like it, but it's close to orange. That's what you said you wanted."

"No, it's perfect," I said. I couldn't tell her. She didn't know. "I love it."

I wore the shirt to school on Monday. She was so proud of it. She thought she'd really done well. I appreciated it, but I dreaded getting on the bus in that shirt.

"You look so handsome. All the girls are going to love you," she said over breakfast as she admired the shirt.

And I appreciated that she bought it for me, that she wanted to give me the things I wanted even though we couldn't afford them. I popped the collar of the shirt and still felt some amount of swagger. I wore the shirt a few times and nothing happened. Maybe I'd pulled it off. Maybe no one looked close enough to see the fox. A week or so later I wore the shirt again and a boy I didn't know passed me in the hall and coughed "piker." I never wore the shirt again. When Mom asked me why I hadn't worn it in a while I told her it had gotten too small.

"I told you," she said. "I knew you were due for a growth spurt."

When it came time to get the winter clothes out and put away the summer, we took the shirt back to the Nearly New so some other kid could wear it in shame.

The Nearly New hadn't changed all that much since I was last in there. It still looked like a store that had been inserted into a room that was built to be something else, a half-assed retrofit that never smoothed out. Before I was born, the place had been a Five and Ten. The outline of the soda fountain was still etched into the tile floor to the left of the front door. The metal shelves were piecemeal—some beige, some white, some brown, the powder coat chipped away in places. I entered the store and cut to the right, away from the cash registers and the klatch of old ladies browsing a display of plastic Thanksgiving yard ornaments.

Thanksgiving. It dawned on me that the holiday was two days away. I turned away from the old women, who had noticed me staring at them and moved closer together as if proximity to one another would offer them some kind of protection from the scary man: me.

The men's clothes were near the back of the store. Closer to the section, the musty smell of long-stored clothing crawled into my nose, laced with mothballs and mildew. First, I browsed the shirts, hoping to find a good western snappy deal, but there was nothing but quilted flannels and out-of-date dress shirts with collars wide enough to land a plane, a couple of gas station attendant shirts stained beyond redemption with grease. There were packages of new T-shirts—white only. I couldn't bring myself to take anything off the rack. I moved deeper into the section looking for the outerwear.

"Can I help you?"

I didn't hear the woman come up behind me. I turned quick, startled, and she flinched a little. I recognized her as one of the old women gathered around the Thanksgiving decorations.

"I'm looking for a winter coat," I said.

She looked me over. I couldn't figure out why she seemed so nervous until I caught a glimpse of myself in a full-length mirror at the end of the row. My hair was smashed in on one side, a wave of greasy thatch, my face unshaven for I couldn't remember how long, the beard patchy and graying on the chin, road rash on the side of my face. Once again, it took me a full two or three seconds to connect the man in the mirror with myself.

"Just this way," the woman said, keeping her distance as she moved around me. I'm sure I didn't smell all that great either, but she made a good show of not crinkling her nose. As we approached the racks she said, "It's getting a little late in the season. We don't have a lot of selection right now."

"I'm sure I'll find something. Thanks so much for your help." I was trying to be overly polite to compensate for my outward appearance. I watched her retreat down the aisle and rejoin her friends who had stopped their conversation to watch her deal with me. I scanned their faces, feeling like I should know them, they should know me, but they were unfamiliar.

She wasn't kidding when she said there wasn't much to choose from: a couple of ski parkas with the stuffing coming out, two or three sizes too big, a cheap-looking blue satin Moose Lodge parka with Earl embroidered over the left breast. The only jacket my size was a hunting jacket with a leaf pattern camouflage and patches of blaze orange on the back, shoulders, sleeves and chest. I slipped it on and it fit perfectly. I checked my look in the mirror. Ridiculous. But it was warm and the price was right: only five bucks. I slipped it off and made my way to the counter. I passed a display of long underwear and picked up three packages. I hadn't worn long underwear since those winter days I spent with Dad at the cabin when I was young. It was clear I was going to need them again.

The women watched as their friend once again braved interaction with me. Our transaction went smoothly. I took the plastic bag from her and thanked her for the help.

"Have a blessed Thanksgiving," she said and I told her to do the same.

Outside, the day had warmed up a little. I put the new clothes in the van and sat in the driver's seat wondering what I should do with myself. Drinking the day away was still in the back of my mind. I tried to keep the thought right there. I wanted a shower, but there was nowhere I could think of to do that. I couldn't imagine spending the rest of the day on the hill with Dad. I listened to the clock in the dash tick away the minutes. My stomach growled. It was lunchtime. What I really wanted was a pepperoni roll, another one of the Italian delicacies native to the area. The story was that Italian wives used to bake these rolls for their husbands to take into the mines instead of sandwiches and eventually the other miners wanted to eat them too, so the wives started baking in bulk. When I was a kid you could get a pepperoni roll just about anywhere: bars, gas stations, the supermarket. I had a pepperoni roll, a Little Debbie and a can of Coke every day for lunch all the way through high school. There was a woman who had a little store in the downstairs of her house and she sold exclusively to the high school kids. For an extra quarter you could get a scoop of canned chili inside the pepperoni roll, which was about as close to heaven as food could get. Just thinking about it made me want a pepperoni roll more than anything in the world. I decided to try the VFW, a few blocks down the road. I wasn't sure they would let me in, not being a veteran, but I had to give it a try. I put a bar of motel soap and my toothbrush in my pocket, too. Maybe I could clean up a little if the bathroom wasn't too bad.

The place looked much the same as it had when I

came there with Dad, a stout cinderblock building painted beige, flat roof, gravel lot to one side. Behind were the railroad tracks, next door was the old depot falling apart, all the wood window frames rotted, the windows gone, the brickwork blackened. There had been a fire.

I parked in the gravel lot and sat there for a few minutes reading the names on the bronze plaque bolted to a stone that sat at the edge of the lot. I recognized some of the last names, but none of the firsts. No one in Vandalia I knew personally had died in a war. I looked at the building. I was nervous. The last time I'd been there was that day before the hunt when Dad beat the hell out of that guy. Part of me felt twelve years old still wanting to run ahead of Dad but holding myself back, matching his gait. I cut the engine and went to the door. The buzzer was still in the same place, worn by years of fingers until there was a hole in the center that revealed the little light bulb inside. To my surprise, the bulb still glowed. I jammed my finger into the button and waited. A few seconds later the door buzzed back and I pushed through.

The same ammonia and cigarette smell, but this time it was familiar to me, almost welcome. I looked down the bar and saw a couple guys sitting a few stools apart, both of them staring into their beers. Neither one of them looked up as I passed. The old jukebox was gone, replaced by a newer one that played CDs. There was a pool table in the back, but this had all its legs. Things were on the rise at the VFW. I sat at the corner of the bar and took a long look at the two other guys, thinking I might know them, but I didn't. They were nameless, faceless bar stool buzzards. Either they didn't notice me looking or they didn't care. Their faces flickered in the blue light of the TV hung above the bar. Wheel of Fortune was on. The bartender waited for me to get settled on the stool and then came to me.

"You a member here?"

"My dad is."

"Who's your dad?"

"Ford Martin."

"I didn't know Ford had a son."

I flinched. That hurt. "I haven't been around for a while."

"What are you drinking?"

"Bud."

He went to the taps and came back with my beer.

"You want to start a tab?"

"Sure. You got any pepperoni rolls?"

"Yeah. You want it zapped?"

"Yeah."

He went to the other end of the bar and took a pepperoni roll down from a shelf. Just seeing the bread, the thin plastic wrapper, made my mouth water. He threw the roll in a little white microwave and turned the dial. He watched the oven until the bell dinged and then he drew the roll out onto a paper plate and carried it to me steaming.

"I haven't seen your dad around lately. What's he got himself into?"

"He's sick."

The bartender nodded his head. "Nothing too bad, I hope."

"Cancer." I said it just to see how it sounded out loud.

"Jesus. That's too bad. I'm real sorry. He going to be OK?"

I shrugged.

He stared into a space somewhere between the pool

table and the jukebox and didn't say anything for a long time.

"Your dad was just a couple years ahead of me in school. I remember watching him play football. Lots of folks...well, I always liked him OK."

"What's your name?"

"Nelson. Nelson Franks."

"I'm John," I said. I held out my hand and he shook it.

"You come back home to look after him?"

"Something like that."

"That's a good boy. I hope my boy would do the same for me. But you know how it is: kids grow up and get into their own life and it's hard."

"Yeah."

"You tell your dad I said hello."

"I'll do it."

He went down the bar and filled the glasses of the other two guys. He looked back at me a couple times and I pretended to be concentrating on my pepperoni roll. I couldn't enjoy it. I washed it down with the second half of my beer and waved to Nelson for another.

I spent the rest of the afternoon drinking beer and watching game shows with the sound off. By the time the sun went down I was good and drunk, numb and happy. It wasn't a bad way to be.

There's a certain liberation to knowing that you're drunk enough that you can't drive. It frees you to keep drinking. It frees you of any responsibility you might have had for the day before you got drunk. I knew the trade off was a night sleeping in the van or finding a woman to take me home. I'd done both plenty of times before and six or eight beers into the day I could handle either. There was not a single woman in the place though. I thought about this as I watched Jeopardy. I watched the answers come on the board and spoke my questions under my breath. I never knew if I was right, except for Final Jeopardy, which I got wrong. I went to the jukebox and slid two dollars into the slot. I was drunk enough to want to get sentimental and I wanted to hear some Waylon and maybe have myself a good cry. I was the only guy in the place now and the bartender sat at the other end of the bar doing crossword puzzles. He looked up every few minutes to see if I needed a refill. When I did, he came to the end of the bar and filled my glass. We had a good thing going.

I paged through the CDs on the jukebox and was disheartened. No Waylon at all. Some Johnny Cash, just a greatest hits. There was actually a Celine Dion record in there. Most of the rest of the CDs were by guys in hats who looked more like underwear models than country singers. I went for a few Johnny Cash, an Allman Brothers and a couple Skynard songs. I let the songs play out, not really listening and waved to the bartender to get something else to eat. Maybe some more food would get my blood sugar into the black and brighten the mood.

"What else you got to eat?" I said. I was slurring now. I heard it and he did too and he gave me a quick sideways look to see if I was going to be trouble any time soon. Inconclusive. I really wanted a chili dog.

"We only got pepperoni rolls, chips and pickled eggs."

"What kind of chips you got?"

"Potato, Dorito, and barbecue pork rinds."

"I'll have another pepperoni roll, and pork rinds."

He brought them to me. My beer was almost empty. I drained it and pushed the mug toward him.

"Why don't you have a Coke or something?"

"I want a beer."

"You've had plenty. It won't hurt you to have a Coke."

"You're not going to serve me?"

"I didn't say that. I just said maybe you should slow it down a little."

"You my mother now?"

He picked up my glass and put it in the sink.

"Take it easy. I know you've got some things on your mind, but I won't let you sass me in here. You sass me and you're out the door."

I took a deep breath. I didn't want to go down that road. I looked at the food in front of me. I took another breath.

"Fine. Bring me a goddamn Coke."

I ate the food and drank the Coke and did feel a little clearer in the head, but the damage had been done. The place was starting to fill up with guys coming in after work. No one was really paying me any attention, but I'd seen a few guys looking at me with a territorial glance that said once they got a couple in them they were going to poke me to see if I'd squeal. Mostly, I just felt too drunk and sad to deal with it. I finished the food, left a few dollars on the bar and walked out looking at the floor, not wanting to start anything. It was still early and I needed a fresh venue.

It was full dark outside. How long had I been in there? Must have been over five or six hours, but it didn't seem like that long. I stumbled a little getting to the van. No way could I drive. I breathed deep. The air was cold, but I was warm in my new coat. I actually felt a little happy. I looked at my reflection in the window. The jacket was comical. I laughed at myself. It was somehow my father's face. Not my father now, or as I had known him when I was young, but the man he must have been in those years I didn't know him. I flattened my palm on the window to block out the face and pushed away from the van.

There was no traffic. Somewhere a few streets away I heard a pick-up gear down and gun through town, but all around me it was quiet save the murmur of the terrible country music coming from inside the VFW. The railroad tracks were just beyond the edge of the parking lot. I went to them and looked down the line. We used to put pennies on the rails and wait for the trains to come by and flatten them. The story was if you put too many on the tracks at one time you could bring the train off the rails. I once put twenty-two on to see if that would do it, but the train kept going. I collected the pennies and laid them on top of one another, then wrapped them in a rubber band.

The tracks were rusted. It didn't look like trains came through here at all anymore. There was still coal to haul out wasn't there? Maybe there wasn't. The depot was burned down. I started to walk the tracks, heading out of town. The night air cleared my head some and it felt good to be out under the sky. The dusk had gone blue-black, like a bruise. I searched the sky for stars. I didn't know many of the constellations, but I recognized the North Star, the Big Dipper. I followed them across a train trestle. I was always too scared to cross the trestle when I was a kid, nothing but open space between the ties. It could swallow me up. The other kids crossed though. There was a tree fort on the other side and to be a member of the club you had to cross with your eyes closed, no peeking. I never did, and they laughed at me as I stood there trying to will myself across. The boys disappeared into the woods and I was left to walk, slump shouldered, back home.

The trestle seemed so small now. The space between the ties was a few inches, not enough to fall through, whereas back then it seemed like miles, a chasm to cross dozens of times over. I crossed easily and headed on, past the footpath that led to the tree fort. The path was still beaten down. Kids must still have a fort in there. There had to be other kids who couldn't cross, too.

I walked for maybe twenty minutes, feeling my way in the growing dark. I saw an open space ahead of me, off to the right. I don't know why I didn't recognize where I was—I had been there many times before—but something about the angle coming from the tracks and not the road made it hard to gauge. At first, I thought a tornado had cleared a big patch of forest and I was seeing the broken white stumps of the downed trees, but as I got closer I recognized the cemetery. Mom used to bring me here with her twice a year to leave new plastic flowers on the graves of her parents. I'd never met either of them. They died before I was born and I always got the sense that Mom came there out of duty and not love. I once asked her, "What were they like?" and she said, "They were good people." That's all she ever said and I knew she was saying that because she didn't want to tell me the truth.

I hopped the fence and it came to me that Mom herself was in there somewhere.

It wasn't hard to find Grandmother and Grandfather's graves. Their headstones were more weathered than I remembered. They were sandstone, not marble or granite, and crusted with bird shit. No one was left to keep them up. Their names had begun to melt away. I could still make out Thomas and Harriet, Father and Mother, the dates.

Harriet had been a schoolteacher before she married Thomas and from the way Mom talked she'd always resented having to give up her career, but that was a time, and Vandalia a place, where women didn't work if there was a husband to provide. She took her frustration out on Mom. I know she made her do twice the schoolwork that the other kids did. She was Mom's private tutor. As a result, Mom was a very smart person, but resentful of what she knew, or maybe how she came to know it. When the time came that she could decide what to do for herself, she didn't go to college; she went to secretarial school instead and married Dad before she finished. I think she married Dad out of rebellion. He was from the other side of the county, the working side. Grandfather—Mom's dad—was an accountant for the coal company. There was a huge divide between these two strata.

She met Dad when she was nineteen. He was in the Army, not long out of high school himself. I've seen pictures of him in his uniform and he looked like the buzz-cut Army-era Elvis, tall and lean, a slightly hooded brow that made his face intense, his eyes a little smoldering. It's not hard to see why a girl who had never had much freedom and desperately wanted to break from what held her down would see this guy on leave from the Army—white T-shirt with the sleeves rolled, a pack of Winston's visible through the fabric, jeans cuffed over fresh, shining Dingo's—and fall in love immediately without thought of the consequences. I think they did love each other, too, for a while. I could see that in the early pictures, them smiling, touching each other, comfortable. It wasn't until several years later when the faces in the photos started to look tired, the smiles strained, the space between them small, but miles wide at the same time.

I don't remember ever seeing them kiss.

It was so quiet in the cemetery. I always loved that. I pulled some of the weeds around Grandmother and Grandfather's graves and propped up the flowers. Plastic roses bleached of all color. There wasn't really much I could do for the graves of a long dead and forgotten couple.

I expected Mom to be somewhere nearby. She wasn't. I walked further into the cemetery, toward the back, where it looked like they had cleared some trees to make room for fresh residents. The headstones out here were a little more plain than their older counterparts. The dates were more recent and I followed them forward in time until I came to the year when Mom died. I walked through the rows and found her midway down the third row for that year. Her stone was small, about three feet wide, a foot and a half deep, eight inches tall. It read: Gail M. Halter-Martin, November 13, 1941-May 23, 2000. That was all, no "Mother," no poem or Bible verse, just the facts of her birth and her death, a perfunctory rose carved into the gray stone beside her name. No flowers, plastic or otherwise, anywhere near her. I sat down on the grass beside her and stared at the stone. I wanted to say something. I felt sorry for a lot of things, but mostly I couldn't get away from the thought of her dying with no one there for her. Guilt. Was she angry with me for not being there? Did I make her sad? I saw myself for a moment as she must have seen me: gone, lost, damaged. How could I have not called her more often? How could I have not told her I really loved her before she died. Who sold the house after she was gone and what happened to the money? Would she have left it for me?

A flush of excitement jolted me again when I thought about having a big check waiting for me down at the bank.

And then more shame. Always serving myself.

I let the sounds of the cemetery come to me, the rustle of the nearby woods. I looked into the tree line and saw a flash of orange, two reflected pinpricks in the dark. Cat's eyes. There was something out there watching me. I kept my eyes on the place where I'd seen the flash and waited for the animal to move.

Minutes went by and nothing. Was it a mountain lion stalking me? "Painters" people around here called them. Had it come out of the woods somewhere further down the lane, now working its way up behind me? Fear got me off the ground and moving toward the main gate. Every sound was now the animal tracking me, preparing to pounce. I looked back several times at the woods and didn't see the eyes again.

CHAPTER 6

The cemetery was about a mile and a half outside of the town center. By the time I got back, I was sober. What to do? Drive back to the truck and sleep or continue the night? I'd cleaned up a little in the VFW, washed my face and pits and turned the T-shirt inside out so it didn't look too dirty. I'd wet my hair and pushed it back. Its greasiness was doing a good job of keeping it there. The clock above the bank drive-thru told me it was only seven o'clock. Too much time to stare at the ceiling of the camper and listen to the woods creeping in. Plenty of time to get myself into trouble. I checked my look in the plate glass. Hillbilly suave. The new coat was growing on me. The old anxiety built up in me and I let it take over. When I came to Front Street, I remembered the old punk rock bar and thought I'd check to see if it was still around. Before I left town it had closed for a while when the owner just disappeared one night. Some people said she was killed by Rastafarian pot dealers (there were a lot of Rastas in the area back then). If pot were legalized tomorrow, I think it would become the number one cash crop in West Virginia. There were rumors of huge fields of pot hidden throughout the hills. Kids ruminated over finding one of those fields and plucking a lifetime stash, but the rumors included Rasta attack dogs, shotguns and the resolve to deploy either or both to protect the crop. There were rumors that Stella, the owner of the club, was mixed up with drugs somehow, but no one could prove it. Then one day she was just gone. Maybe it was drug biz gone bad, or maybe it was she just wanted to get the fuck out of Dodge.

I played my first gig with my high school band there. We were called Vital Signs. It was a terrible name. I walked through town sure that I would find the bar boarded and long defunct, like everything else in town, punks not being the most effective business people in the world, even if booze was probably the most successful business to be in around there. But as I rounded the corner, there it was: a neon Guinness sign in the window, no placard outside announcing the place's name, same as it had been when I played there even though I was too young to legally go inside. David Bowie wafted out the door: "Kooks." I stood outside and looked at the flyers stapled to the board, same as it had been all those years ago, as if I'd really gone back in time. I scanned the band names and didn't know any of them, but the flyer art was still similar to what it had been before. I pushed through the door feeling good that there was something about home that still remained as I remembered.

I settled at the corner of the bar. There was no one else in the place but me and the bartender, a guy who looked familiar to me the way people do in music clubs. He was about thirty, maybe a little older, band T-shirt over a small beer gut, jeans in need of a good washing, Doc Martins. He was reading a copy of *Tropic of Cancer*.

"Hey," he said and then waved his hand over the taps and bottles to display his wares.

"Guinness," I said.

He bowed and went to the tap. He pulled the Guinness in the proper way and I watched the foam cascade down the sides of the glass while he made my change and laid it on the bar. He lingered for a second and I could tell he had a question. I met his eyes.

"You look familiar," he said.

"I used to live here when I was a kid."

"You ever been in here before?"

"When I was seventeen. My high school band played here a couple times."

He nodded. I couldn't tell if he was someone I knew or not. I didn't think so.

"You from around here?" I said.

"Nope. I went to school for a couple years in Morgantown and then I came up here to live at The Farm."

"What's that?"

He jerked his head toward the door. "Place out off Bolyard Road. A bunch of folks live out there. Kind of a commune or something, I guess, but not all hippied out. We grow some food and in the summer we have a little festival. It's cool."

I knew the place he was talking about. It used to actually be a farm when I was really young. The Bolyards had been out that way for long enough that they had the road named after them. We used to buy cantaloupe, tomatoes, and pumpkins from their roadside stand. Old Mrs. Bolyard was a scary woman. She had big moles on her face and it always made me a little ill to look at her. The cantaloupes were good though.

"Sounds cool," I said and he drifted back to his book. He looked a little old to be reading Henry Miller. I went through that phase when I was twenty-two, I think. I didn't have any urge to read him again. That kind of stuff—Miller, Kerouac, Salinger—was best experienced young, remembered fondly, and never relived. I tried to re-read *Catcher in the Rye* when I was thirty and couldn't get through.

I downed the Guinness. It was good—thick, almost black, sweet molasses and bitter fruit. They served it in the English style; warm in an imperial pint glass. I hadn't had a Guinness like that since New York. It used to be my celebration drink. When something went well for the band I'd go to the pub on Grand Street just off the corner of Bedford and drink Guinness. I loved that bar in the summer. There was a little garden in the back and I'd sit on a plastic deck chair under a trellis that hung from the building behind and watch people come and go. Summer is a glorious time in New York. A lot of people flee the hot weather, the sticky heat that clings like a damp mildewy wash cloth, but for those who have nowhere to go, the great unclean scrappers, there are pleasures to be found. The girls in Williamsburg wore fewer and fewer clothes as the summer unfolded, until it seemed all there was to see were beautiful, young wannabe-something girls in wife beaters, braless, wandering through the bars as aware of my reverence as I was happy to give it.

The place started to fill up as I finished my third beer. I dangled my glass at the bartender and when he came over I asked him what was going on tonight.

"Open mic," he said.

I looked at the collection of people milling around, cupping beers in their hands and I recognized the nervous tension that comes before taking the stage in folks who haven't done it all that much. I've felt it myself. It's made worse by the burning desire to give off the vibe that you'd rather be anywhere than in that particular place at that particular time, doing anything else.

I decided to play the open mic. I hadn't been onstage in over three years, since the last band gig that ended with me drunk after the label rep told us they weren't releasing the record.

I sat on my stool and watched the first few acts, got drunk again, and got that old feeling, that "I'm ten times better than these losers" itch. A couple of them were OK, but there was one guy who got up and did a couple of his own songs who really got me going. He had a good voice and the folks in the crowd were with him right away. By the time he got to his third and final song the crowd was whooping at every glissando of his voice. I couldn't take it. There's something about open mics. On the surface they seem like a sad exercise in letting the untalented play act at being rock stars, but when you get some talented people in the room who are playing the open mic because they are just getting started (like this guy—young, pretty and talented) or who are on their way down (that would be me), it can become an epic ego pissing match for the soul of the room. I couldn't stop myself. I was back at the VFW parking lot and digging my guitar out of the van before I'd even thought about it.

Here's the funny thing: Regardless of what happened or didn't happen in my "music career" I have never doubted that I'm good. Sounds like a bit much, I know, but there it is. When I was about six, Mom took me to the mall to buy school clothes and as we walked up and down the halls I sang as loud as I could, whatever song came to mind. Mom was embarrassed. People turned their heads and grinned at me, gave Mom that knowing glance that said they understood she had her hands full with a boy like me. Finally, she couldn't take it anymore. She pulled us out of the flow of traffic and asked me, "Why are you doing this? You're making everyone look at us."

"I have to do it, Mom," I said. "If I don't sing then how will I be discovered?"

She looked at me for a long moment like I was not her son. It's not that she didn't like that I could sing or that she discouraged me from it, but no one in my family had any kind of musical talent at all, so on some level no one knew what to do with me. Not that I wasn't trotted out at family gatherings to be the performing seal, but I liked that, so I didn't complain.

The bar had gotten comfortably full in the time it took to get my guitar. I went over to the sound guy, who was also running the list of the performers. I was signing up late, so I was far down the list. I had maybe five people to wait through before it was my turn, but it was still pretty early. The young guy had made a very costly error. He shot his wad when the room wasn't yet full. I'd have the benefit of a full room of people who'd had a few drinks. I settled back at the bar and waited my turn; a smiling Buddha prepared to dispense some wisdom.

When my turn came the sound guy called my name from the board and I walked to the stage, I didn't make eye contact with anyone as I wove my way through the crowd. I didn't know any of these people and I wanted to give off the mystery man vibe. I stepped onto the mottled, sticky carpet and set my case down. I unfastened the latches on the case and drew back the lid. My heart jumped a little, just at the sight of the guitar. It was beautiful, a Gibson Hummingbird that I bought new when I got my advance check from the label. It cost almost $3000. I ran my fingertips over the sunburst top, the oversized pick guard with the intricate hummingbird design etched into it. I read somewhere once that an instrument is a magical thing because before someone takes it into hand, it's nothing but parts, wood and wire, but then, somehow, the player breathes life into it and makes it into something it isn't. I love that idea. I've never felt more at peace than when I have an instrument in my hand and my voice is about to snake its way out of me. I realize that I am like the guitar, nothing but parts until the voice comes out of me. I have spent my life in service of the voice. The times in between when I am onstage, singing, I am in the case waiting to be played again, just like the guitar. I gave it everything I could to bring life to the voice so it could stand on its own, but I failed. All I have left are those tapes and a knot in my stomach when I think about what could have been. But the longer I move away from that time, the more I know it wasn't going to be what I wanted it to be. It was the carrot, but the race was what mattered and now the race is over. I'll have to live with that for the rest of my life.

I took the guitar out of the case and swung the strap over my head. I hadn't even had the thing out of the case in almost two years. A pick was still slotted between the strings just below the nut. I fretted a G chord, leaning close to check the tuning over the din. Still in tune. After all that time, still in tune. Like magic. The soundman was standing at my elbow.

"You need a mic for that?" he said.

I shook my head and dug a patch cable out of the case, right where it had always been. I let it unfurl and handed one end to the sound guy. The other end I slotted into the guitar. He hopped off stage and I checked the mic, the guitar. He gave me the thumbs up.

I was nervous. My mind blanked and I started playing the first song I could think of, one of my own, called

"Could It Be Me?" It was kind of an upbeat song, a straight rocker with some rockabilly feel in there, too. It was a good opening song. I opened most of my sets with it and it was the opening track of the album trapped on the tapes in the van. I let the first eight bars roll into sixteen, trying to get the feel again. Just as I rounded the chord progression coming to the turnaround I felt it: the voice was there. I was ready. I stepped to the mic and looked at the crowd for the first time. Some of them had already noticed there was someone a little beyond a regular Open Mic Joe on the stage. I drew in a breath and let the voice come.

By the time the song was over I had them all. No one in the room was talking, every eye was on the stage. The bartender had even stopped pouring drinks and come to the end of the bar closest the stage. I felt wistful and sad that I could do that, that that was in me, the pointless transient power of it.

The next song was another one of mine, a slower tune called "Leave It Alone." The silence in the room deepened. A few women moved closer to the stage, a few couples paired up and danced. I took an extra turn through the progression before hitting the last verse to give the dancers some more time together. The applause at the end of that song was even louder than for the first. I scanned the room and saw the guy who'd made me jealous before watching from the bar. He leaned in and said something to the bartender who shrugged in reply. He wanted to know who I was.

I finished with "Ain't No Sunshine" by Bill Withers. Not a lot of people know it, but Bill Withers is from West Virginia. I was shocked when I first found out. I always loved that song and I sang it well. It was a good set closer and it did what it needed to for this little set. I'd worked out an arrangement for it where I could use the voice for maximum effect, drawing out parts of the last verse and then smoldering over the coda. When I stopped there was no sound in the room but the coolers behind the bar humming. The silence lasted two or three seconds before everyone exploded all at once with whoops and applause.

I packed up the guitar and ignored the people who were trying to get my attention at the lip of the stage. This was part of the act, too. I was all business, trying to get myself cleared off the stage to make way for the next performer. I hopped down and finally smiled at the small group of people huddled around me. Most of them said good job and stuff like that, some offered to buy me drinks and I followed them to the bar.

What ensued was one of the more drunken nights of my life. Two or three Jaeger shots made their way into my hand within the first couple of minutes of leaving the stage. The young guy I'd set out to put to shame came over and we chatted a little. He seemed like a nice kid. Another college dropout living on The Farm. He asked where I was from and I told him I grew up in Vandalia but had spent a decade or so trying to make it in New York. He was impressed. He wanted to go, he said, try to make it. I didn't have the heart to tell him it probably wouldn't be worth it if he did, one way or the other.

I spotted a woman, older than most of the folks in the bar. When I first saw her floating at the edge of the group my drunken heart jumped a little. "Who is that woman?" I said to the guy beside me.

"Where?"

"She was over by the jukebox."

"What's she look like?"

"Someone I used to know." I was too drunk. I thought for a minute it was Crystal, my high school love. The girl I lost my virginity to, who was going to run away to New York with me, who ran away from me before we could go. I spent the first few years in the city trying to find her and the next half a decade trying to forget it. It wasn't her. I knew that, but I wanted it to be. I couldn't put the words together to describe her.

The kid slapped me on the shoulder. "I don't know man. You're wasted."

"Yeah," I said. "Fuck yeah I am." Someone put another shot in my hand and I gulped it down. She reappeared at the edge of the stage.

I stared for a while longer, trying to place her. It took a few minutes but finally I realized she was the stripper from Dan's club, Mist. Her face was scrubbed clean of makeup and she wore a bulky wool shepherd's sweater, faded jeans. She was probably thirty, I could see now. Beautiful. She saw me looking at her and moved toward the bathrooms. I had to talk to her. I downed my drink and waved for another. I stood at the mouth of the hallway where she had to reemerge once she finished her bathroom business. Five minutes went by. Nothing. More girls came and went. I stopped one and asked if there was anyone else in the room. She shook her head, "No." I went down the hallway. There was a door that lead into a parking lot behind the place. She was gone. I went to the bar for another drink.

The bar closed down and I was in the bed of someone's truck, bouncing through town, hugging the guitar case for dear life—it's life, not mine. The night air cut through the drunk just enough for me to be embarrassed of the cammo coat and my greasy hair falling in my eyes.

We drove out of town into the woods. The truck stopped. There was a fire in a field.

"So you really played in New York? How hard was it to get gigs up there?"

"It's easy, man," I said. "Keeping them is hard." I laughed and the people around the fire laughed with me.

The fire is dying. We're surrounded by singlewide trailers, old school busses, campers, huts that looked made of sod.

Hands lifting me, leading me away from the fire, holding me up as I get sick in the brush.

"Where's guitar?" I say through thick lips.

"It's OK." A woman's voice.

"I'm sorry, Mom."

The sun silvers the sky to the east.

"Beautiful," I say to it.

CHAPTER 7

Awake in the wan light of early morning, quiet around me. Wind through the trees. For a second I thought I'd somehow made it back to the camper. I was still a little drunk and that was for the best. If I slept another couple hours I'd be immobilized for the whole day, but as it was I could ease my way down.

I remembered little bits of the end of the night. I remembered riding in the truck. I remembered the bonfire. That was about it.

Panic.

I shot up too fast—queasy, head pounding—and looked around the room. Where was the guitar? Can't lose that guitar. Goddamn it. I was in a trailer. Bowed wood paneling arcing away from the wall, an old black and white TV. A sewing machine set up on a stand on the other side of the room, one of the old kinds, non-electric, with a foot pedal. Overstuffed armchair that matched the couch where I'd slept, slick velour, brown and vaguely forest themed. It was cold in the room. There was a wood stove by the door, the flue exiting the place through an after-market hole in the wall, fiberglass insulation stuffed into the space to keep the outside out.

The guitar was leaning against the wall on the other side of the front door. Relief. I was still dressed. Good, I guess. I stood slowly and tested how hungover I was. Not bad for now, but I had to get another drink in my belly before it got worse. I looked around the room again, out the window at the empty field, at the structures littering the ground. The Farm. I went to the guitar and opened the case.

Everything was right where I'd left it.

I found a beer in the fridge. I opened it as quietly as I could and downed it fast. It settled my stomach. The growing pressure in my head dialed down. I had to pee.

Down the narrow hall there were three doors. The bathroom was the first, so I went in and let the stream flow. I was louder than I wanted to be, but it felt good to let everything out. I heard movement behind me and stuck my foot out to kick the door shut. Piss sprayed the carpet and the wall behind the toilet. The door only closed halfway. I refocused and finished, trying to ignore the figure that stood in the door watching me. I buttoned up and turned to the door.

A boy, maybe twelve or thirteen, stood in the doorway. He had dyed black hair, one side of his head was shaved. In the eyebrow opposite the shaved side there were three earrings. He wore a black T-shirt advertising a band I'd never heard of—at least I thought it was a band—and stretched out tightie whities. His eyes were narrowed, his lips pressed tight together. We looked at each other for a few seconds, me in shock, and him with the purest hatred I'd ever seen.

"You missed, fuckwad. Now it's going to stink." He turned away from the door and went back into the room where he'd come from. A few seconds later, loud hard-core punk blasted through the thin walls of the trailer.

I tried to remember more of the night before. Hazy half-images of the bonfire and people passing a joint around came to me. The beer had helped with the oncoming hangover, but it wouldn't help for long. I needed to either get some more sleep—preferably a whole day's worth—or some more beer. Either way, I'd be fine. That wasn't going to happen in this trailer. I started to calculate how long it would take me to walk back to town as I pulled my boots on. The other bedroom door opened.

"Thanks for letting me crash on your couch," I called. I was afraid to see who else might live in the place. "I'll be out of here in a second."

I turned around to smile at my host and I nearly fell over. The stripper, Mist, stood in the opening of the hallway, leaning against the doorjamb. She wore a thick cotton robe, the vague suggestion of a flower pattern still visible through many washings. Her hair was a thatch of fire. Neither of us said anything for a minute.

"You were pretty wasted last night," she said after a while. "I'll cook you something to eat before you go."

She moved through the room barefoot. I looked at the floor. I didn't know what to say. I still wasn't convinced that she was really there.

"Thanks for taking me in." I followed her into the kitchen. My head protested. My stomach flipped over. I stopped in the doorway so I wouldn't puke on her floor.

"I have a soft spot for strays." She said and took a carton of eggs from the refrigerator and broke two into a plastic bowl. Whisk-whisk-whisk-whisk.

"I saw you last night. I wanted to talk to you."

"Why would you want to do that?"

"I don't know; to apologize, to flirt with you. I played at the open mic. I was feeling pretty good."

"I saw you play. You were pretty good. Is that what you do?"

"It's what I used to do."

"Why used to?"

"Long tale of woe. You don't want me to get started."

She stopped cooking and looked at me for a second. "Whatever."

"What's your name?" I said. "Your real name, I mean."

She scooped the eggs. No answer.

She didn't say anything for a long time. Outside the window the hilltop was a wasteland of broken down dwellings. "Anna," she said. Her voice was soft. I wanted to bury my face in her hair, smell the dank musk of her pillow still trapped in there. Suddenly, I didn't want to ever leave this trailer. I wanted to hold her, this woman I didn't know. I reached out and touched her shoulder. She stiffened and slipped away.

"Don't."

I drew back. "Sorry." She couldn't have been more different than her club persona. Mist was confident, surly, invulnerable, but Anna was none of those things.

She carried the plate to a small Formica table by the kitchen window. There was a small plastic pot on the edge. It held withered basil plants. She took the pot from the table and dropped it in the garbage without saying anything. I started to eat and she stood somewhere behind me either watching me or looking out the window. I stayed focused on the food. The first few bites were hard to keep down, but once they settled I wanted more.

"Thank you," I said when I was done. "I needed that."

"No problem."

"And thanks again for taking me in. You didn't have to."

"I know."

I wanted to hear something encouraging in her "I know," but her tone was flat, no inflection. I couldn't find anything in her voice. She was cooking more eggs.

"What's your boy's name?" I said.

"Francis."

"Really?"

"It was his grandfather's name."

The eggs were burning. She stared down at them, not turning toward me, not stirring, just looking.

"How old is he?" I asked.

"He's thirteen," she said.

"Seems like a good kid."

She took the pan off the stove and threw it in the sink, turned the tap on, walked out of the room, down the hall, and closed the bedroom door behind her. I looked around. Everything was different, like there had been a subtle shift in reality.

The punk music still roared from the other bedroom. I wasn't familiar with the song. I listened for a minute to the muffled, unintelligible voice. I couldn't make out a single word. I turned the water off and looked at the eggs, the pan, the dirty dishes in the sink. I braced myself against the counter and hung my head as a wave of nausea rumbled through my gut.

Another beer from the refrigerator. I drank it fast. I was shaking. The song ended and another started, the same tempo, the same onslaught as the song before. I tried to think of myself at thirteen. What was it then? Michael Jackson? *Thriller*? Still the Beatles? I owned *Thriller* on every media: Cassette, 8-track and LP. I wore that thing out.

I felt loose inside. I wanted to leave, to walk out of the trailer and not look back. I sat down on the couch and put my hand on my forehead. The warmth of it felt good. It was still cold in the trailer. I pulled the blanket over my shoulders and breathed deep, trying to stop the shaking. She wouldn't have covered me if she didn't want me there. She wouldn't have taken me inside when I could have passed out somewhere in the woods and died. I wanted to die. And I wanted to live. For the first time in a long time, I knew I wanted more.

When I woke, the boy was standing over me, arms at his sides, fists clenched. I was startled and for a moment I didn't know where I was. I made a sound, like "ooh," and he laughed at me.

"You're such a loser," he said.

I worked my way to a sitting position. "What gave it away?"

"Don't think you can stay here."

"I don't."

"Good, 'cause I'll kill you."

"Why would you do that, Francis?"

"That's not my name."

"That's what your mother told me it was."

"She's not my mother."

"Who is she then?"

"The whore that dragged me into the world."

"Not your mother though?"

"No. I'd have to love her for that." He crossed his arms and stared out the window.

"Interesting distinction."

"Fuck you very much."

I rubbed my temples. "You certainly are a charmer, Francis."

"If you call me that again, I'll slit your throat."

"You'd be doing us both a favor, kid."

He looked at me for a second with his head cocked

sideways, like a dog that just heard a curious sound. The door to the bathroom opened and Anna came into the room. She looked completely different, hair not combed, but tamed somehow, the robe gone and in its place a snug v-neck sweater. Kelly green. Old jeans. Face not made up, but scrubbed, cheeks red, brightening her sad eyes.

"Leave him alone, Frankie."

"Bitch," Frankie said under his breath.

"Back to your room and don't come out until you can be civil. And no music."

The boy tromped out of the room and slammed his bedroom door. Anna looked at me and smiled. She shrugged. Her demeanor was so different from a couple hours before that I couldn't be sure if I'd dreamed our previous interaction.

"Are you hungry?" She smiled at me again. A completely different person. No recognition of the scene from before. I played along.

"Sure." I stood, waiting for the wave of pain, but it didn't come. The sleep had been just what I needed to fend off the hangover, but sometimes the pain laid low, waiting until I made a sudden move. I turned and watched Anna scrape the burnt eggs into a plastic garbage pan. She didn't remark on them or make any excuses. She was hitting the reset button. I took a couple steps and still felt all right, so I let myself move to the kitchen entry and I leaned on the partition, doing my best James Dean.

"Thanks again for last night," I said.

"You were pretty messed up. The people out here are OK, but most of them are so screwed up themselves that they don't look after each other. I saw you passed out by the bonfire alone after the hootenanny broke up and I knew you'd be dead by morning if I didn't get you inside." She cracked two eggs and put them in the now-clean pan.

"Well, still."

"You're welcome."

I watched her cook. She moved with the absent-minded efficiency of someone who had performed those actions a thousand times. The way she handled the implements of the job made me think she'd spent plenty of time working in a kitchen for pay.

"You want some bacon?" she said. My mouth watered at the thought of it.

"Sure."

She took a package out of the refrigerator, not a store-bought plastic sleeve, but a big hunk of pig wrapped in butcher paper. She took out a long knife and sliced off a few strips, again with the acumen of a professional. I watched her work. It had been a long time since I'd seen bacon like that. When grandmother had pigs that's how she kept her bacon. I was back in her kitchen again on an early Sunday morning, watching her cook, already halfway done up for church. Anna dropped the bacon into an iron skillet.

"How long have you been in town?" I said.

"Going on three years. We bounced around a lot for a while, after Frankie's dad left. I met him early, married early, had Frankie too early. I had a friend who came out here to the Farm when they first started the place. I had nowhere else to go, so I came."

"Where are you from?"

"Down in Boone County. I came to Morgantown to go to college. I got a scholarship for dance. I thought I was going to New York and get a job on Broadway or something. Instead I met Kevin and I was pregnant by the end of my sophomore year. It didn't matter anyway. I wasn't that good a dancer and I hated studying. When I was a little girl I just loved to do it. As soon as they made me work at it I lost interest." She turned the bacon.

"I know what you mean. I tried to study music for a while and felt the same way."

"You are really good. I meant that."

"Thanks."

"What happened?"

"What do you mean?"

"Why don't you do it anymore?"

"Nothing."

"What do you mean 'nothing'?" she said after I was seated.

"Just that. I lived in New York for a long time. I played in a band. I got a little record deal and then the company dropped us before the record came out. I don't even have the rights to the recordings." I'd never said any of that out loud. I was too afraid that saying it would make it true. There with Anna I could say it. I was relieved.

"And you just quit?"

"I didn't quit."

"You're not in New York anymore. Are you still doing it?"

"No."

"Why not?"

"Well, because everything fell apart. I worked all that time and I had nothing to show for it."

"So you quit."

I was getting mad. I didn't want to get mad. This was the first time in a long time that I was around a woman who made me curious. I wanted to stay right where I was.

"There are no second acts in American lives," I said.

"Fitzgerald was a self-important windbag. That's all bullshit."

I laughed.

"What?" She was getting mad now. She thought I was laughing at her. "I've read a few books. Sometimes the package doesn't exactly advertise the contents."

"No," I said. "I know. I'm sorry."

"You still didn't answer my question."

"I don't know the answer. I woke up one morning and thought about where I was, what happened, and I just felt tired. I couldn't do it anymore."

"So you quit."

I chewed a forkful of eggs. I wanted the conversation to end. "I guess I did," I said.

"Good for you."

"Why do you say that?"

"You got out of the way of the people who won't quit."

"Easy for you to say."

"You don't know anything about me."

"That's true."

The rest of the compound was waking up. A young woman in a calico dress came out of a camper across the field and picked up a green plastic bucket. She disappeared around the back of another trailer and then a minute later I saw her walking toward the tree line. There was a fenced-in sort of barnyard. I hadn't noticed it before. There was a lean-to with three stalls that housed a couple cows and another structure that looked like it was made of shipping pallets. It had a little ramp that went to a small door and when the girl—it was clear she was younger than I thought she was at first—made her way through the gate a brood of hens stumbled out the door. They gathered at her feet and she sprinkled feed.

"What are you doing here?" Anna said.

I had forgotten where I was again, back in my mind to Grandmother's house, the feel of the eggs when I took them out of the nests in the thin white light of a morning, still warm, the shells soft. When I squeezed them they gave a little and that feeling scared me.

"I don't know. I guess someone dragged me back here last night after the bar closed."

"Not here. Here." She waved her arms around like she wanted to encompass more than The Farm, meaning Vandalia.

"I grew up here."

"Really?" She seemed genuinely surprised.

"Yeah, really."

"You don't have an accent."

"Now look who's judging a book."

She laughed. "Yeah, sorry." She took a glass bottle of milk out of the refrigerator.

"I never had one. I don't know why. My dad does. My mom did. I just didn't. Maybe it was because of the singing."

She nodded and looked out the window. The girl was coming back from the chicken coop now, her bucket heavy with eggs.

"Your mom passed away?"

"A couple years ago."

"Sorry."

"It's OK."

"Your dad still around here?"

I nodded.

"That's good. My parents are still down in Boone

County, probably plotting ways to kill each other."

"Could have been worse; they could have got divorced."

"It would have been a blessing to all of us."

"Don't be so sure. The grass is always greener, but sometimes that's because the grass is growing on a big pile of shit."

She laughed at that. I was getting my charm on. The food had brought me back to life a little. It felt good to hear her laugh.

"I'm guessing your parents got divorced."

"Yeah."

"Who did you live with?"

"My mom."

"How did she die?"

"Car crash."

"That must have been hard."

I didn't answer. I didn't want to tell her the truth. I didn't want her to know what kind of shit-heel I really was. She was starting to like me and that felt good. We were quiet again.

"I'm sorry if I pried," she said.

"It's OK. You didn't. I just don't like to talk about it."

"Where were you before you came back here?"

"Arizona. I was working as a maintenance man at a motel."

"Why'd you leave?"

"I hit the glass ceiling," I said. "Nowhere to grow."

"Right."

"Honestly, I don't know. I didn't feel like I belonged. I've never really felt like I belonged anywhere. When I left Arizona I thought I was just moving on to the next place and the next thing I knew I was back here. I left when I was eighteen and told myself I'd never come back. I hated it here. I hated everything about it."

"If it's so bad why do you think you came back?"

"I've been wondering that myself ever since I got here. If I had to come up with an answer I'd say it's because I really had nowhere else to go. I ran out of options."

The conversation lulled. She did the dishes. I moved to the sink to help.

"I've got it," she said. I sat down at the table and watched her work. When she finished, she dried her hands on her pants and looked out the window.

She went into the bedroom and came back with a small duffle bag. "Get your stuff," she said. "I have to go to town and then go to work. I'll drop you wherever you need to go."

"My van's at the VFW."

"Classy place."

"It holds sentimental value."

"Figures." She chuckled a little when she said that, which made it sting a little less and gave me some hope.

I followed her out the door to a beat-up pickup. She dropped her duffle in the bed. I climbed in the passenger seat and held the guitar between my knees.

"Do you like your work?" I said.

"Don't be a jerk."

"I'm not trying to be. I'm curious. I want to know more about you. I want to know why you do that. You're smart. You could do something else."

"And all strippers are dumb?"

"No, I didn't mean that."

"That's what you said."

"Sorry."

"You should be."

"I'm going to shut up now," I laughed and she watched the road. We came to town. I didn't have much time left before we got to the van. I didn't want to let her go.

"Can I see you again?" I said.

"No."

"Why not?"

"Because you seem like you're a pretty nice guy, but fucked up and needy and I already have a teenager to deal with. No offense."

"You know, when people say stuff like 'no offense' they always say it right before or right after something offensive."

"Yeah, well, it softens the blow."

"Not really. It's kind of offensive."

She looked at me. Her eyes were hazel going on gold. "Yeah, I guess."

"What if I came to see you at work?"

"That wouldn't be a good idea."

"Why not?"

"Do you not remember how that turned out the last time? Our bouncers are like elephants; they remember."

"But I'm a friend of Dan's."

"Not if he finds out you stayed at my place."

"But nothing happened."

"That doesn't matter. He's a cokehead and an egomaniac. He'll beat the shit out of you himself."

"But I'd do it just to see you again."

"There's no point. I don't want to see you."

"I think it would be romantic. A story we could tell our grandkids."

"We won't be having any of those."

"You just don't see my good qualities yet."

"Oh, I see them, they're just not enough to outweigh the bad."

"You're a hard nut to crack, Ms. Anna."

"Don't bite down too hard or you'll break a tooth." She stared at the road ahead.

"You've got to give me a chance."

"I don't want to."

Her voice was straightening out, getting more and more tense. I didn't want to push too far, so I just let it go, but in the back of my mind as we turned onto Front Street I was considering ways that I could see her again.

It started to snow. The snow drifted like ash over the windshield and we rode in silence. I wanted to say something more to her, but I was afraid that if I spoke she would close up forever. She was a woman with a teenager and more troubles than she knew how to deal with and I couldn't blame her for not wanting to add to those troubles with someone like me. We pulled into the VFW lot and I got out. I left the door open so she couldn't drive away before saying goodbye. "I really appreciate you taking care of me last night."

"I wasn't going to let you freeze to death."

"Still, thanks."

"OK."

"I really want to see you again," I said.

"You are a pushy sonofabitch."

"Is that a yes?"

"It's a 'No.' Why can't you just accept it?"

"I have a hard time with 'No.'"

"You should apply some of that attitude to what you do with that thing." She pointed at the guitar.

She got me. I looked at the ground.

"Close the door," she said. I did. She backed out of the lot and drove back the way we came. I thought for a second about following her, but I felt sad again and just stood there for a while leaning against the van with the guitar resting against my leg. For a second I hated the guitar so much I wanted to throw it into the ravine beyond the railroad tracks. Instead I listened to the wind moan through the empty street. There wasn't a soul around. It was Wednesday.

I took my time getting back to the camper. I had the same feeling I had when I went to visit my grandfather in the hospital after he had heart surgery—a kind of excitement at the new surroundings of the hospital and a dread that death was around every corner, a fear that it could be coming for me. I got to the truck and at first I couldn't get it to start. I was careful not to flood the engine and waited a while after my third try, just listening to the sound of the woods around me. I tried to identify everything I heard and could only name a mourning dove. I knew that Dad would know every sound, and there was a time in my life when I would have, too. Even though I didn't spend all my time growing up there, I knew it. There aren't many places in the world where you can say that. I thought about how the land no longer belonged to us. It was someone else's land. How can generations of work, of connection, be gone in one transaction, erased by one mistake? It was easier than it seemed it should be.

The truck started. I guided it out of its hiding place and went deeper into the woods. It was dusk already. Where had the day had gone? How long did I sleep that second time? It was hard to know. I thought about Anna again. There was something about her. I did like her but I didn't think she would let me close enough. But then why had she taken me in? There must be something there.

Dark under the trees as I climbed the hill. For the few minutes it took to drive to the top I actually felt pretty good about things. I was giddy, in that euphoric moment when the hangover starts to clear. The pale light of the fading winter day seemed right to me. I was glad I'd come home. I didn't know what was coming next, but I was ready.

It was dark inside the camper and I couldn't see much as I came in. "Dad," I called out, but there was no reply. I moved into the room and saw him lying on the bed, just as I left him. Nothing in the room had changed. I called to him again and he didn't respond. Panic. My heart started pounding. I went to the bed and touched his shoulder. He was facing the wall. I could see even in that low light that he was pale, more pale than before. Or was it just that I hadn't seen him in a day and misremembered? I put my hand on his ribs. They moved with a shuddering breath. "Dad," I said again. He moved his lips but no words came out, just a sound almost like insects moving inside a wall. I didn't know what to do. He was worse than before. He was dying. It was the first time I really thought about that as a reality. He was dying. I said it to myself, moving my lips but making no sound. I sat down at the table and watched him. From that distance, in the half-light of the darkened camper, I couldn't see his breathing. The urge to run was strong, but I couldn't leave him there. Or I wouldn't, at least not this time. I'd spent too long running and it was time for that to be over. I had to do something. I couldn't bear the thought of waking up in the morning with him dead in there with me.

I looked at the form on the bed. He had been such a

big man to me when I was young, but the person on the bed there was so small, so thin. I thought I could put him in a bag and carry him. I tucked the quilt tight around him. He stirred a little and tried to say something again, more like words this time. "Another piece of cake," I thought he said, but it was so faint and there was no way for me to know.

I lifted him. His bones stuck out at every angle, an elbow in my ribs, shoulder blade digging into my forearm. I thought of the dream I had when I was a boy. This was the dream. I wanted to wake up. Wake up, wake up, wake up, I said to myself over and over as I carried him to the truck. He whimpered when I put him in the seat. He couldn't stay upright and I seatbelted him in so he wouldn't slide off the bench. Was he still sleeping? Or was he in a coma? Should I just let him go? All I knew was that he wasn't there with me and suddenly I wanted him back.

The hospital was a huge limestone building that sat on the top of a hill just outside town. The place started life as a TB sanatorium in the early 20th century and in the fifties the main building became the hospital and the rest of the land was sold to one of the coal companies. They thought there was a big vein in the hills above the hospital, but there must not have been because the woods were still there along with a collection of old cabins where the TB patients used to stay. The place looked like a cross between a summer camp and a concentration camp. When I was a kid, we used to go up there to make out. I could see the outline of the cabins through the leafless trees, dotting the hill like stone outcroppings.

All the way through town I kept an eye out for the cops. It was hard to keep from speeding through town, but I held back. The ride was the longest of my life. I put my hand on his back to be sure he was still breathing and I talked to him the whole way. I wanted the sound of my voice in his ears, as if that would keep him with me.

I parked underneath the emergency canopy and carried him through the big sliding doors. The nurse behind the desk saw me coming and held up a hand to stop me.

"You can't park there." She raised herself half out of her chair. She was a stubby, round woman. Her midsection strained the buttons of her uniform. I could see pale skin through the gaps.

"I'm not parking. I have an emergency."

She looked from my face to the bundle in my arms. Her expression changed, like she just noticed I was carrying a withered, unconscious human.

"What happened?" She started doing something with the computer behind the counter. She picked up a telephone and held it to her ear with her shoulder. She paged a code over the PA system.

"I don't know. I came home and he wouldn't wake up. It's like he's in a coma or something." It felt strange to me that I had just called the camper home, but I pushed past the thought. Focus. The nurse came out from behind the desk and wheeled a gurney around. I laid Dad on the thin pallet as softly as I could. He didn't stir. "He has cancer," I added.

"Name?"

"Mine or his?"

She pursed her lips. *'I don't have time for this,'* her look seemed to say.

"Ford Martin," I said

"Who is his regular physician?"

"I don't know."

"What medications is he taking?"

"He won't take any."

"Allergies?"

"None that I know of."

"What kind of cancer does he have?"

"I don't know. He said it's everywhere."

She wrote these things down on a form.

"When was the last time he was in to see a doctor?"

"I don't know. I only came home a few days ago. I hadn't seen or talked to him in a long time before that."

She nodded and wrote a few more things on the form. A group of hospital workers rushed through a set of double doors at the far end of the hallway and descended on him. A dark-skinned man huddled with the nurse and she showed him the form while they talked with their heads close together. He nodded, looked at me and then went to Dad. Another nurse took his blood pressure. It was hard to tell what they were doing. All at once they wheeled him away and disappeared through the double doors again.

"What's going on?" I said. The nurse stood there with me and watched them go.

"The doctor will evaluate your father and let you know what's going on as soon as he can."

"Is he going to be all right?"

She looked at me for half a second with very sad eyes. I could tell that it had never been easy for her to answer those kind of questions. I wasn't delusional. I knew Dad was sick and wasn't going to get better, but I needed to ask the question anyway.

"Just take a seat. When there's something to know, I'll tell you. You just have to be patient."

I walked toward the seats slump-shouldered when she

called to me again, "While you wait I'll need you to move your vehicle to patient parking." She pointed toward the other side of the building. I didn't want to leave the waiting area. For the first time in a long time, I didn't want to run. I wanted to stay right where I was.

I parked the truck under an overhang of trees. It was a nice evening, cold but not too cold. The next day was Thanksgiving. I was back in school again, listening to Mrs. Waycaster instruct us to write down what we were thankful for in our lives. What did I write down? Mom? Dad? My favorite toy? The Beatles? What did I have to be thankful for now? I wasn't dead? Dad wasn't dead yet? There was really nothing to list. Mrs. Waycaster would be disappointed. She would tell me to think harder, try harder. Everyone has something to be thankful for. I hadn't thought about her in years, but I could hear her voice as clear as if she were speaking to me from the passenger seat. "There has to be something, John. If there's not, you're not trying hard enough." She was right. I wasn't trying hard enough.

I didn't want to think about that. I would think about it tomorrow. As it was, I didn't know if Dad would make it to the morning. I walked back across the lot to the emergency room. The pudgy nurse had retaken her post and was paging through a magazine as if nothing had happened. How could she be so insensitive? I stopped myself. These people see this every day. How many dying men had she watched come through that door in the last month alone? Two dozen? A hundred? I couldn't blame her for not batting an eye when we walked through the door. We all come through those doors hanging by the thinnest thread, praying that someone will pull us back. There is no other possible outcome. Everything in between is just filling time.

I drew my coat around me and watched the nurse read for a good five minutes. The cold felt good. The longer I watched, the more it seemed like I'd never been in there, that it had been someone else who had carried his wasted, dying father through those doors, like I'd watched it on TV. No, it was me. This is me. I turned away from the doors and looked out over the valley. The thin glow of the sodium lights made town a mini-sun rising into the hills. I was shaking. I hugged my arms and rubbed, but couldn't stop. I went back inside.

The nurse looked up as I came through the door, ready for more action, but when she recognized me she smiled and waved like we were co-workers passing in the midst of the long slog of another night's work. I took the corner seat in the waiting room, where I could see the nurse and just a sliver of the door where they'd taken him. It was quiet. There was a TV suspended above the chair at the end of the row to my left, but it was turned off. I stretched my legs out and slid down in the seat as much as I could. I took a deep breath and closed my eyes. I'll just rest a few minutes. They'll be out soon with news. I just need to rest.

CHAPTER 8

The doctor woke me, softly rocking my shoulder back and forth. For a second I didn't know where I was. "Who is it?" I said.

"Mr. Martin? It's Dr. Gupta. I'm sorry to wake you. I need to talk to you about your father."

I sat up and rubbed my face. "Is he going to be all right?" There was the question again. It was the same doctor who had wheeled Dad away. He smiled at me when I asked the question, a sort of sad smile, the kind of smile reserved for a child who has asked a question and won't be able to understand the answer.

"Your father is very sick," he said. "I'm afraid he'll get better, but he will not get well." His voice was soft and sing-songy.

"What's wrong with him?"

"Your father has pneumonia. A complication with his cancer. We have intubated him and he is receiving intravenous antibiotics. Once they take effect he will get stronger and he should be able to communicate."

"When can I take him out of here?"

"That's impossible to say. He is very sick. Patients at this stage of the disease...it's just very hard to say. We need to see how he responds to treatment."

I could tell he was hedging, using doctor-speak to work around what he didn't—or couldn't—say: Dad might not leave this place at all still drawing breath. "I know," I said. "I'm sorry. I know you can't guarantee anything. It's just he didn't want to come to the hospital at all. If he was conscious, I never would have got him here."

"That's quite common. I understand." He put his hand on my shoulder again. What brought him to this place, in the ass-end of nowhere? He wasn't young. This probably wasn't a brief stop for him on the way to a better job.

"Can I see him?" I said.

"Of course. He's resting quietly now, but you can sit with him until we move him to a room."

He led me through the double doors and down the hallway to a larger room partitioned by green curtains. Dad was the only person in the room, but they had him screened off anyway. The doctor pushed the curtain back and I faltered a little. Dad had a huge plastic tube jammed in his mouth and there were wires running everywhere. I was scared shitless but impressed with how quickly the doctor and his team turned him into what looked like a huge power strip.

Dr. Gupta waved me into a seat beside the bed. "If you need anything, you can call the nurse. She's just down the hall. If there's an emergency, press this red button." He indicated a button just above the bed on the side where the chair was stationed.

"Thank you," I said.

"Just be patient and stay strong. This is difficult, I know." He smiled again. He patted my shoulder and walked away.

I sat down in the chair beside the bed. I didn't know what to do. It had to be late. I looked around but there was no clock. It didn't matter. I was sitting there until something happened, until Dad woke up or didn't. I wanted him to wake up. I looked at him there in the bed, the slight rise and fall of his chest, the slack skin on his face. He was dying. There was no way to get around it. Throughout most of life it's easy to think that there is enough time for everything, to say what needs to be said and do what needs to be done. I just wanted him to wake up and talk to me. I thought about all the hatred I had for him in those years after the divorce, how I blamed him for everything that happened. I caught myself forgiving him and wanted to stop, but I couldn't. The nurse came in and checked one of the monitors and wrote something on the clipboard at the end of his bed. She smiled at me too as she walked away. Were they trained to do that?

I hate hospitals. Always have. That's not a unique emotion, I know. The first time I remember being in a hospital was not long before Mom and Dad split up. The principal came to my class room and whispered something in Mrs. Waycaster's ear, the two of them looked at me. I tried to think if I had done something and couldn't think of anything. I was a good kid, and it wasn't in my best interest to draw attention to myself. Mrs. Waycaster told me to go with the principal. I could feel all the kids looking at me. Someone said, "Oooh, Johnny's in trouble."

We went back to his office and he sat me down and explained as much as he knew: that there was an explosion, that he didn't know if my dad was OK, that Mom was coming to get me. I looked at him while he talked. I didn't know what to do. We looked at each other for a long time and then he opened a drawer in his desk. He rooted around for a few seconds and then came out with a Dum Dum sucker. He held it out to me without explaining. I'd never thought of him as anything more than the man who stood above us as we filed in and out of the school in the morning, the man who seemed to relish the opportunity to use his fraternity paddle on the deserving asses of rule-breakers.

I took the sucker. I didn't want to eat it. I was thinking about Dad and trying to understand what was happening.

"You can eat it if you want," the principal said.

"That's OK."

"Are you scared?" he said.

I shrugged and looked at a snow globe from Ocean City on his desk. It had a crab inside. The water had gone murky.

"I'm sure everything will be fine," he said. "Your mom should be here any minute. You want to go wait outside?"

He led me out of the school. The two of us stood under the awning where the first, second and third graders lined up before school. I could hear kids playing volleyball inside the gymnasium. The principal and I stood there and watched the road. We didn't talk anymore. For a guy who made his living as a teacher he seemed really uncomfortable around kids, but I couldn't blame him, given the circumstances. He didn't know what was going on any more than I did.

I saw our powder blue station wagon coming around the corner. "There's my mom," I said.

He put his hand on my shoulder and walked me down the stairs. Mom took the turn into the cul de sac too quick and the principal tightened his grip, ready to pull me back if she lost control. The car ground to a stop, kicking a little gravel. I could see the fear in Mom's eyes and I knew Dad wasn't dead. Somehow even at that age I knew that there would be a different look in her eyes if he was dead. I was relieved. I didn't want him to die. I got into the car.

"He's OK," she said. "He's going to be OK." Mom's hands were shaking so much that the seat and floor were dusted with cigarette ash. We didn't talk the whole way to the hospital. She just kept saying, "He's OK."

They already had Dad in a room and the nurse at the front desk gave us the number. The doctors had given him something for the pain and he was sleeping when we came into the room. Mom pulled a chair up to the bed and touched his arm. She was still crying but trying hard to keep quiet. It was the most I'd seen them touch in a long time.

The doctor came in and took us out in the hallway where he told us that Dad was going to be fine. He was up in one of the smoke stacks when the explosion happened and fell a couple stories onto a catwalk. He hurt his back and broke a couple ribs, but he was lucky to be alive. Mom cried more when he said that.

Dad woke up later that day and did his best to act like nothing happened, but I could tell he was hurt. I never saw him hurt before.

"Get me the hell out of here," he said to Mom and started pushing the blankets off.

"Stay there, Ford. Don't do that. The doctor said you need to rest."

"I can't stay in here. People die in hospitals. I'm not dying." He winked at me and tried to smile, but the pain was still there. Somehow he got himself off the bed and made Mom help him dress. A nurse came in, and then the doctor, but no one could stop him. He got his work pants on and his shirt, which he left unbuttoned. He yelled at the nurse and she backed off. I was a little scared, too. We got him home and in bed, where he stayed for two weeks. He refused to take any medicines; he just waited it out. Then he went back to the power plant to work.

It occurs to me now that it wasn't long after that things changed, maybe a little at a time, but they changed.

He started building the cabin that next summer and a little more than a year later he was gone. After he married Maggie he quit the power plant job and never held another full time job as far as I know.

I fell asleep in the chair. Sometime in the night, a nurse woke me.

"We're pretty quiet tonight," she said. "You can crawl in the bed next to him if you want." She pulled the curtain aside so I could see the bed. I thanked her and climbed onto the mattress.

"You want a blanket?"

I didn't answer. She laid a rough polyester blanket over me and turned the lights out as she left. I watched Dad breathe for a while by the light of the instruments and the red glow of the exit sign. It wasn't long before I was asleep again.

The doctor was checking Dad when I woke up. I had no concept of what time it was. I felt like I'd slept for a year.

"How is he?" I asked.

"It's still hard to say, but he seems to be breathing better. It will be a while before we really know anything. You should be patient."

I sat up. Dad didn't look any different than he had when I brought him in. Maybe there was a little more color in his face, but not much. I wanted to ask the doctor another question, so that I felt like I was doing something, but I didn't know what to ask. He looked over the machines and made notes in the chart. He was a small man. I hadn't noticed that the night before. He was balding on the crown of his head. He moved from place to place quickly, sure of himself. He knew what he was doing. He put the chart back and looked at me. He smiled. "Your father will be resting for a while. You should feel free to go out and get yourself cleaned up, enjoy the holiday. Be with your family. If anything happens, we will call you."

"Thanks," I said. I didn't want to get into the fact that Dad was all the family I had and that I didn't have a phone. This man clearly lived in a world where both of those things were givens. He walked away and I sat looking at Dad for a while. "Are you going to wake up, or what?" I said. He didn't answer.

A different nurse was on duty at the emergency desk. I startled her when I came through the doors behind her. She was watching some people talk on TV. Behind them was a New York City street. I recognized it as 34th and Sixth Avenue. They were talking about the parade that would happen sometime soon. I glanced at the clock in the waiting room. Not quite 8:00.

"Can I help you?" she said.

"My Dad's in there."

"Is everything all right?"

"That doctor said it would be OK if I went out for a while."

"Of course. Is there a number where we could reach you?"

I started to tell her no, but thought for a minute. I asked for the phone book and gave her the number for the Kwik Stop. Boulder was the only other person I knew of who was still living and in town. The store would be open regardless of the holiday. Unless things had changed a lot since I was a kid, he'd still be living in the little back room. I wrote the number on a Post-It. If the nurse thought it was strange that I had to look up a number to be reached in case of emergency, she didn't show it.

Jason T. Lewis

I went out to the truck and instead of getting on the road, I sat for a long time and looked at the hospital. I was seeing it both the day of the accident at the power plant, when we drove there not knowing if Dad would come out alive, and in the present, when I knew for a certainty that he was not likely to come out alive. It came to me that I didn't know him. I didn't know him at all. For the better part of my life, the part where you figure out most of what's what, he was not there. The twelve-year-old version of myself had an idea of who he was but that boy was too young to know anything real about people—real concerns, real lives. I saw him then as part hero, part bogeymen. I tried to think of something he'd taught me, anything I got from him that a father teaches to a son. Hunting. That was all. A skill I never used again. The other life lessons, the clichéd rites of passage shared by father and son, he wasn't there for any of them. I learned how to drive a car from a stranger, a teacher making a few extra dollars teaching summer school driver's ed. Driving on the highway for the first time, the teacher pointed out how to line the front fender up with the line on the side of the road to know that you're lined up straight. I wondered if Dad knew that. There was never a birds-and-bees discussion. I learned about women by trying to tune in the Playboy channel while Mom was out on Saturday nights. The first time I jerked off I didn't know what I was doing. I had the channel dialed in and I could see streaky blue breasts and I touched myself. It felt good. I touched myself some more. Then I came. I thought I'd broke myself. I started crying. I went to the bathroom and washed. I took a shower. I was afraid the creamy junk would never stop coming out and I'd have to explain what happened to Mom. But everything was all right. I figured it out. I hadn't really

141

needed Dad, or Mom for that matter.

But part of me knew that wasn't true and it didn't matter. I was here now and he needed help. So I would stay and do whatever was needed.

I thought maybe I was wrong about the Kwik Stop being open when I pulled into the lot. The place was dark and the only car in the lot was a moldering pickup just visible around the back. The door was locked. I knocked a few times on the window. Nothing. I moved to where I could see the cash register and the door that led to Boulder's room. I hadn't been in the Kwik Stop for a long time, years before I left town even. After I stopped seeing Dad I didn't go in there, afraid I'd run into him, afraid Boulder would tell me something about him that I didn't want to know—that he was doing well wherever he was, that he was happy, or that he and Maggie were having a new baby, or that he was hurt, or dying, or dead. I didn't want to know any of it.

Looking through the window I saw that nothing much had changed from the last time I was in there. I hadn't seen Dad more than once or twice in that year but I was getting older; I didn't miss him as much as I did when I was young. Dad picked me up early on a Saturday morning. On one hand, it felt just like any other Saturday that was his weekend. On the other hand, I knew Maggie would be at the cabin waiting for us. I hadn't given much thought to him being married to her up to that point.

That Saturday morning I remember thinking for the first time it was real: Mom and Dad were never going to get back together. Maggie and him were married. I was too old to be still thinking like that, but I couldn't help it. There was some part of me that thought if they just got back together then Mom would stop drinking and Dad would come alive again and we would be happy. I was angry with myself for wanting it at all. I hadn't said a word since we got in the truck and Dad let me be quiet for a while.

"I need to stop at Boulder's before we get up the hill," he said. "Maggie needs a few things."

My back stiffened at the mention of her name. "OK," I said.

"You doing all right?"

"Yeah."

"Everything good with school?"

"Yeah."

"Your mom still with that guy?"

"Which one?"

"I dunno. The one from a year or so ago, Steve?"

"Stan. No."

We pulled into the lot and I followed him in the store. When I was a little kid I loved coming into the Kwik Stop. I was always guaranteed two things: a free sucker or a Popsicle and to get my pants scared off by Boulder. He knew how to throw his voice, but he could only do it barking like a dog—a little dog, like a Chihuahua or something. It was a game we played. He'd see us coming and hide somewhere in the store. I'd walk in, waiting, telling myself I wouldn't jump when he barked, but I did every time.

Dad and I took a seat at the little lunch counter. There was no one else in the place. No sign of Boulder.

"You want something to eat?" Dad said.

I shook my head. I was still full from breakfast. Mom liked to overdo it when I was going to see Dad; bacon, biscuits, gravy, whatever I wanted.

"You want a Coke?"

I shook my head again. Dad reached over the counter and slid the door on the cooler there. He pulled out a beer and worked the cap off with the opener nailed to the side of the cash register.

"You mad at me or something?"

"No."

"You're not saying much."

"I'm OK."

"We haven't got a chance to talk about Maggie."

"I don't want to."

"You're going to like her. She's a good person."

"OK." I scraped at some dried food on the countertop.

"That's all you got to say?"

"What do you want me to say?"

"I don't know." He paused. "Something."

"Everything's OK."

Then the barking came, right behind me, just like always and just like always I almost jumped off the stool. Boulder cackled from somewhere deep in the aisles of the store.

"Got you," he said. "I got you again." He came out of the refrigerated section and slapped his knee. He was always so proud of himself when he made me jump.

"Yeah, you got me," I said.

"Aw Ford, look at this one. He's got too big to have any fun. Look at that sour puss." He ruffled my hair. I'd recently started to try and comb it into a style and I winced and shied away. "I bet this curly mop goes over with the girls. You getting any use out of that thing there?" He took a poke at my crotch and I jumped off the stool. That got both Dad and him laughing.

Boulder said, "You want anything to eat, Johnny?"

I shook my head.

"Where you been keeping yourself? I haven't seen you in a dog's age."

"School." I shrugged. "You know, stuff."

"Stuff. Ford, you know what stuff?"

"I do not." Dad drained his beer and reached over for another. Boulder slapped his hand.

"A little early for that isn't it?"

"You my wife now?"

There was an edge of real anger in Dad's voice.

"Well," Boulder pitched his voice high, "I like you and all, but I don't swing that way."

Dad reached over and took the beer. Boulder didn't stop him.

"What are you boys getting into this weekend?"

"I thought we might get out in the woods," Dad said. "How's that sound?" he asked me.

"I dunno," I said.

"You don't want to? If not, that's OK."

I waited a long time before I answered. I'd been afraid of him before, but suddenly I wasn't as afraid.

"Not really," I said. "I don't really like it."

That ended the conversation. Dad went back into the aisles and came back a minute later with a package of tampons. Both Boulder and I looked at them and Boulder turned to me, wanting to make a joke, but I pretended I didn't notice. Dad stood at the register and looked down. "How much?" he said. Boulder took the tampons, put them in a sack, and tallied the bill.

"Five even," he said. Dad pulled a pile of wadded bills out of his front pocket and unfolded a five on the counter.

"You have a good one, Ford," Boulder said. "You boys

keep yourself out of trouble."

Dad went to the door and I followed him. Just as I was about to go out, Boulder threw his voice at me again and I jumped. Again. I could hear him cackling up until I closed the door to the truck.

We were halfway down the hollow before Dad said anything. "You mean that about hunting?" he asked.

I didn't want to answer. I'd said that in the store to hurt him, but with the two of us alone I was losing my nerve. "I dunno," I said finally.

"Don't give me that bullshit. If you feel a way, then say it."

"I thought I liked it at first, but then I didn't. I had nightmares."

"I'm sorry," Dad said. "I didn't know."

I could tell he was sorry, but he was also mad. He had to have been disappointed, but he was trying hard not to show it. I looked at the sack that held the tampons. Maggie was waiting for us at the top of the hill. I didn't want to think about that. I turned toward the window and watched the trees fly by.

I'd only ever met her one time before, at the Dairy Queen on a Saturday afternoon not long after Dad left. He introduced her to me as his friend and I was too young to know what that meant. She brought me a toy truck. I never was one to play with toy cars, and Dad knew that. I couldn't understand why he didn't tell her. I wanted him to tell her. I needed him to tell her, but he just grinned as I took the toy and ran it over the table a few times trying to act like I was excited about it. We ate Peanut Buster Parfaits. I was so nervous and sad that I ate mine too fast, so fast that I made myself sick. I ran to the toilet and threw up the whole thing.

Some of the puke splashed onto my shoes, my favorite shoes. They had little pockets on the sides. I kept a quarter in each pocket and used them to buy Little Debbies from the corner store on my way home from school. I was eleven years old. I wanted Dad to come help me get cleaned up. I opened the bathroom door to try and wave to him and get his attention, but he was looking at Maggie in a way I'd never seen him look at Mom, this kind of sleepy-eyed look. Five more minutes in the bathroom scrubbing my shoes with a paper towel. I got most of the puke off, but there was a ghost of white from the ice cream that I could never really get gone.

They were still mooning at each other when I came out. I asked Dad to take me home and he said he wanted to take me to the park, but I told him I didn't feel like it. He looked hurt, the same kind of hurt he had in his face as we drove to the cabin where Maggie had been installed as his new wife. What was he thinking when he had that look on his face?

I knocked on the window of the Kwik Stop a couple of times and was about to give up when I heard the tell-tale thump of Boulder's uneven gait coming toward the door. I couldn't see him. By the sound of it, the years were catching up to him. His steps were slower than I remembered. It took him longer to drag the heavier shoe along.

"Don't you know it's a goddamn holiday?" he said as he reached the door. He busied himself with the lock. "I was watching the goddamn TV in there." He pushed the door open so I could enter and at the same time reached behind the door for the lights.

"You've gotten grouchy in your old age," I said.

"Says who? Who's that?" He looked at my face and I saw his eyes were clouded over with cataracts.

"It's John Martin, Boulder. You remember me?"

He paused for a minute and then reached for my hand, grabbing it easily and pumping it hard. "Well, there he is: John Martin." He pulled me through the door. "Do I remember you? I'm half-blind, not senile. I remember you, boy. 'Course, you been gone long enough that you couldn't blame me forgetting."

"Yeah, I guess that's right."

He led me to the lunch counter and patted a stool.

"Where you been keeping yourself?" he poured me a cup of coffee and set it on the counter.

"Around. I was in New York for a long time, then a bunch of places."

"New York City?"

I nodded and then caught myself. "Yeah."

"Whoo wee, big city man." He plucked the collar of his stained white T-shirt. "What were you into up there?"

"Tried to play some music."

"How'd that go? You a big star now?"

"Not exactly."

"Well, you'll get it. You always had that in you."

I didn't respond. We were quiet for a minute.

He said, "I was sorry to hear about your Mom."

"Yeah, me too."

"She was a good woman."

"Thanks."

"It was a shame."

"Yeah," I said.

I drank the coffee.

"You have breakfast?" He moved to the griddle and

turned the burners on.

"Don't trouble yourself. I thought you'd be open. I was just going to stop in for a few things."

"I'm not open much these days. They got that new Food Lion down the road in Oakland and I can't compete with those prices. I guess I'm semi-retired. A few folks still stop in for breakfast and lunch, but not on a day like today." He took a package of bacon out and threw four pieces onto the griddle. "You want toast?" He put a couple slices of white bread into the toaster before I could answer. Then he took a handful of hash browns out and threw them on with a hunk of butter. He moved faster than I thought possible, knowing where everything was without looking.

"I said I don't want anything. Don't put yourself out."

"If you're anything like your dad, you haven't eaten."

"I'm not anything like him."

"So you've had your breakfast?" He smiled at me.

"You're still an asshole."

"What kind of talk is that? You should respect your elders, especially the crippled ones."

"You look like you're doing OK."

"I can't complain," he said. "Well, I could, but then no one would come visit me at all anymore." He tended the food in silence for a minute and then scooped the hash browns onto a plate and then the bacon. Everything was perfectly cooked.

He asked, "You seen your Dad?"

"Yeah. I've been staying with him up on the hill."

"Jesus Christ. You know he doesn't own that place anymore?"

"I know."

"What are you living in?"

"He's got a camper up there."

"Old pull-along thing?"

"Yeah."

"That camper doesn't even have heat. What are you going to do when it gets really cold? A man as sick as your Dad needs a bed, someplace warm."

"He said you'd been taking him food."

"I did when he had an apartment in town, but not since he went back up there. My truck won't make it up there and I told him I wasn't going to help him if he was going to crawl off like an old cat to die."

"Jesus," I said.

"He's a stubborn sonofabitch."

"I know."

"But what are you going to do about it?"

"What can I do if that's where he wants to be?"

Boulder faced the window and folded his arms. "How is he anyway?" he said.

"Not good. I had to take him to the hospital last night."

Boulder shook his head. "He going to be all right?"

"What do you think?"

Boulder sighed and wiped the counter with a rag. Outside, there was no traffic on the road. "It's a shame. He wouldn't let anyone help him when Maggie took him to the cleaners."

"You know who she sold the land to?"

"I don't. Developers most likely. This time next year there'll be condos or something up there."

We were quiet again. I didn't know what to say. Everything felt hopeless. I was drowning in it. I tried to picture the hill with real roads, real houses. I couldn't do it. I thought about Anna. I wanted to see her again.

"You still got beers in that cooler?"

Boulder reached in and brought out a Bud. I worked the cap off with the opener that was still nailed to the register stand, right where it had always been. It wasn't lost on me that I was following in Dad's footsteps. I drank the beer fast and felt the rush of the coolness of it. I put the bottle down and took satisfaction in the clunk of it on the counter top.

"Could I get six of those to go?"

Boulder took out a six-pack and put it in a bag. "You got somewhere to go? You got someone to have supper with today?"

"No," I said and then I thought about it a little more. "I don't know. I thought I might drive around a bit. I might just go back to the hospital and sit with Dad."

"You're welcome to eat here with me. I don't have much of a spread planned, but you're welcome."

"Thanks, Boulder. I appreciate it. I just might do that." I put the six-pack under my arm. "What do I owe you?"

He waved me off. "Nothing but another visit sometime soon."

"I've got to pay you something."

He waved again. I looked at the money in my wallet. Not much left. He didn't seem to notice when I put the wallet back in my pocket again.

"I'll see you again soon," I said. "Thanks for the breakfast."

I was halfway out the door when he threw his voice behind me. "*Rararararar!*" I jumped.

CHAPTER 9

I drove the truck back to the parking spot and got in the van. I just wanted to drive, drink the six-pack and try not to think, but I didn't want to take the risk of driving around in an unregistered vehicle. I sat in the van, keys in the ignition, and listened to the sound of the forest around me. It was a quiet that could lull you to sleep for the rest of your life. I opened a beer and rolled the window down, the cold morning air keeping me awake.

I could put the van in gear and pull out, be gone again. There was a time when that would have made me tingle, the idea of a new place, somewhere out there, unknown, but sitting there under those familiar trees, thirty-one years old and feeling like I'd lived a lot longer than that. I was weary. I never knew the difference between weary and tired before that moment. I wanted to crawl in the back of the van and put my head down. There was nothing to stop me from doing it. No one expected me anywhere. I finished the first of the beers and put the bottle back in the six-pack. I twisted the cap of the next one. The beer was making me feel better.

I finished half the six-pack sitting there. By then I was feeling good. I started the van and pulled out to the main road. Then I drove. I didn't know where I was going or why and I didn't want to. I just let the wheels turn. I circled the county, seeing it all new again, but also through the gauze of the past, the vague memories of years before. I came to the Maryland border and I let myself slide over it. I was a little giddy, down to my last beer by that point. I could just keep going. I was free. In ten minutes, I was in Oakland.

The town had always done a real nice job of keeping itself tidy, like a proud old lady who always makes sure her creases are running right before she leaves the house for a trip to the store. It was like the land that time forgot, squat little buildings that still housed businesses that most towns had long run out of use for; a five and ten, a sewing repair shop that sold vacuums, a little bookstore, a pharmacy with a working lunch counter. I was hungry by then and remembered the hamburgers at that counter as some of the best I'd ever had.

I parked a little ways up the block. Getting out of the van, I stumbled a little, drunker than I'd expected. I made a conscious effort to walk straight down the sidewalk to the pharmacy. Closed. Jesus. It's Thanksgiving. What the hell's wrong with me? My stomach was in high gear anticipating that burger. Now I was dizzy, light headed with hunger. Back in the van I followed the main road toward the far edge of town. There among the car dealerships and motels was the Food Lion Boulder mentioned, just where I thought it'd be.

I slipped through the door at 11:45, fifteen minutes before their posted closing time. There was a tubby guy, maybe mid-forties, sitting on a folding chair just inside the sliding doors. He was wearing a cheap-looking security shirt.

"We close in a few minutes." He said it without any conviction. He looked like a guy who used to work with his hands but his job was gone now and he'd been reduced to sitting in the doorway of a supermarket for minimum wage. He looked bone tired. There was a Barcalounger in his near future after a big plate of turkey. I envied him. I could see in his eyes he was already there in his mind.

I nodded and continued into the store. I'd come in with nothing more than a plan to get something to eat for myself. Maybe it was seeing that guy on the folding chair or maybe it was in the back of my mind all along, but a more elaborate plan for the day formed in my mind. I went first to the refrigerated section and picked out a medium-sized turkey, then I swung down the dry-goods aisle for a box of Stove Top, a box of mashed potato mix, a half-gallon of milk, a pumpkin pie, a case of Bud cans, and some whipped cream. I had it all in my cart in less than five minutes. I was feverish, like I was in some kind of dream. I stood in the check out almost shaking with excitement.

Another few minutes and I was back in the van, my loot stashed in the back, heading back toward Vandalia. Twenty minutes later I took the turn off to The Farm, giddy. I pulled into the space beside Anna's pickup and loaded everything into my arms, hoping that the fact that I came bearing gifts would get me past her initial defenses.

I had to put the beer down to knock. Nothing. I thought maybe she had seen me pull up and was playing possum inside. I knocked again, but nothing stirred inside the house. I sat down on the little step to the trailer, not sure what to do. The euphoria of my morning six pack was wearing off and I was faced with a holiday alone with nowhere to go but back to the camper, where I all I could do with these groceries was drink the beer as it got warm and watch the turkey go bad. The Farm was quiet. I could hear the chickens in the coop making chicken noises and it made me think of my grandmother's again.

The trees in the distance swayed in a breeze that hadn't made it to me yet. They whispered some kind of truth so soft I couldn't hear it. Tears threatened at the rims of my eyes, but I was tired of being the guy who cried when no one was looking. I took a beer out and drank it down fast. The burn of the carbonation took away the tears. I dropped the can in the brush beside the trailer and opened another.

An hour passed and three more beers with it. I was feeling pretty drunk when I heard movement inside. I made sure the cans weren't that visible in the overgrowth and then I picked up all the bags again. I knocked on the door. This time the footsteps I heard paused and then moved toward the door. I arched my shoulders back and waited. Anna opened the door wearing her robe.

"Jesus," she said. "I really wasn't kidding when I said I wasn't interested."

"I know. I just...I was having a bad day. I had to take my dad to the hospital last night. I didn't have anyplace to spend the holiday and I didn't think I'd make it through the day alone. I bought some stuff. Will you let me cook for you and Frankie?"

"Looks like you're already halfway to making it through the day." She nodded to the cans in the brush.

"I'll pick those up."

"Fuckin'-a you will."

"Can I come in?"

She stood her ground for a few seconds and looked at me. "I already got a turkey."

"Save it for Christmas."

Finally she stepped aside and I carried my bags thorough the door.

"You can cook dinner and you can eat with us, but you're not staying here. I'm not giving you anything. I meant what I said."

"OK. Just let me into the kitchen."

I set to work, prepping the turkey first. I was glad
I didn't get a big bird. It was already into the afternoon
and getting a turkey of any size started this late meant it
wouldn't be done until supper time or later. Anna left the
room while I worked. I had the oven heated and the turkey
in a bent up tinfoil pan before she was back again, dressed,
scrubbed and still narrow-eyed with doubt.

"You need any help?" she said.

"You can get me something for the stuffing and the
potatoes."

She went to a cabinet and got down a couple of pots
and set them on the counter beside the stove. I went to
work on that stuff, not wanting to talk, as if talking would
scare her off, like a bird that had landed close to me, a bird I
wanted to watch for a while.

I drank another beer while I worked, but was
conscious that I should slow down. If I tipped over to the
real drunk place, things could go really wrong fast. When I
had everything going, I sat down at the small kitchen table
with her. I looked at her while she pretended not to notice.
She really was a very pretty woman. She had small wrinkles
around her eyes that on some women would have showed
their age, but on her they made her look wise. Her mouth
was thin, but her lips were very red, not lipstick red, but like
she'd just been kissed hard. I wanted to kiss her.

"Stop staring at me," she said.

"Sorry."

"You keep doing that."

"What?"

"Staring at me. I've seen that look before. You're seeing
someone else."

I went to the stove to check the stuffing and potatoes. "No."

"Don't lie to me. I hate liars."

I didn't want to talk to her about another woman. I didn't want to tell her about Crystal, but at that moment I was falling, loose from everything all at once. I said, "You remind me of my high school girlfriend, just a little."

"Jesus. What is it with guys and their high school sweethearts?" She threw a dish rag into the sink.

"It's not like that," I said.

"What's it like then?"

"I don't really want to talk about it."

"Too late for that."

I couldn't hide behind cooking anymore. I had to tell her. There was something in her voice that said she'd be gone, inaccessible, if I didn't. I drew a deep breath and held it, then I said, "We were supposed to move to New York together. She was going to Columbia and I was going to be a rock star."

"What happened?"

"You know, the usual; we broke up."

"Not good enough." She moved to the couch and curled her legs under her. She was going to get it out of me.

"She was my first, you know, partner. Well, we were each other's firsts. Junior year. I really did love her. I promised myself I wouldn't have sex until I was in love. And we were in love."

I didn't want to go on. I'd never told anyone any of this.

She laughed. "Sounds like a John Hughes movie. Where'd it all go wrong? Did she fall for a bad boy and dump you? Or did she get to college and realize you were too small town for her?"

I gripped the edge of the counter. She was making me mad.

"No, she got pregnant," I said. I let the words hang there. Seconds passed. "I asked her to marry me," I said. "She said no. She had an abortion, or at least I think she did. She left town and I didn't know where she went. I moved to New York anyway. I spent the first year hanging around the Columbia campus, playing guitar on the sidewalks, hoping I would see her, that the music would draw her to me, I guess. Nothing. I checked with registration. She never showed up at school. I never saw her again. After that, I just kept playing. I played all the time. I didn't know what else to do."

She studied the veins on the back of her left hand. She traced them with a fingernail. The wind kicked up and rattled a loose piece of siding on the trailer. She didn't speak.

"Maybe that's where everything started to get fucked up for me," I continued. Things were fucked up before that. I stopped talking.

"I'm sorry" she said.

"It's OK." I went to the stove and pretended to attend to the food. She got off the couch.

"You all right?" she said.

"Yeah."

"I was being an asshole. I apologize."

"It's all right."

Neither of us spoke for a few minutes. I basted the turkey and turned the gravy down low. She got me a beer from the fridge. We looked out the window, almost touching.

"That's a hard story," she said.

"I guess."

I drank my beer. The day turned toward dusk.

"Where's Frankie?" I said.

"I don't know. He was gone before I woke up. Sometimes he goes out walking. Just when I think maybe he's run away or something he comes back like he's never been gone."

"You mean, like for days?"

"No, hours, but they're long hours. He knows how to make time painful."

"Huh."

"What?"

"That just seems like a sad thing to say about your own kid."

"Well, it's sad but true. He comes by it honestly."

I let the conversation drop for a minute. "Where are the rest of the folks?"

"Who knows? They like to take holidays like this and use it as an excuse to go all pagan, everybody fucks everybody and takes a lot of drugs."

"But not you?"

"Not me."

"Why not?"

"I've been down that road. It's a trip I only want to take one time."

"But you're still here."

"I knew a guy here, the trailer was available. When he took off I stayed. They don't bother me. I think they're scared of me."

"I can see why. You've got a crusty exterior."

"You really know how to charm a girl."

"It's a gift."

She smiled a little.

When the potatoes and stuffing were just about ready I turned the burner down and checked the turkey. It was going to be a while before it was done and the two of us were alone. I didn't want to waste the goodwill I'd built and I was afraid if we stayed in there alone for too long I'd blow it, make a move or say something that couldn't be taken back.

"You want to go out for a walk or something?" I said. She looked at me suspiciously. "Just a walk."

"Yeah, I guess."

We put on our coats and for a minute it was like we'd done that together a thousand times. I felt natural with her. That's something that most people probably take for granted, but I've always had a hard time with it. I usually feel like the person I'm with secretly longs to get away from me at the first chance.

We started out moving away from the old farm house and the other dwellings along an old dirt track that went into the woods about three or four hundred yards away. We didn't talk. The silence was nice, soothing, and after a while we fell into step with one another and just walked. We came to the tree line. There were the remnants of an old barbed wire fence blocking our way, I stepped over a section that had sagged, careful not to let the barbs get my pant leg. I held out a hand for Anna when I made it safely to the other side but she pretended she didn't notice and put a boot on the wire and pressed it down with her weight as she crossed. The old fence sank to the ground and she kept moving like it was never there.

The woods were filled with dusky winter light. We kept moving, not talking until we came to another field stretched up the hill. We walked to the top of the ridge and Anna stopped, looking down the hill to the next stand of

trees that extended beyond where we could see. I looked
to the horizon at the line of hills on the other side of town.
One of them was our hill, mine and Dad's. Or it wasn't ours
anymore.

"What's wrong with your dad?" Anna said. I looked at
her and she was still watching some point on the horizon.

"Cancer."

"What kind?"

"I think it started in his lungs but now it's spread out."

"That's too bad."

"Yeah."

We were quiet again. There was no sound but the
wind in the leafless trees.

"Why aren't you with him in the hospital?"

"He was sleeping. The doctor said it would be OK if I
went out."

"Are you close?"

For a second I thought she was asking if the doctor
and I were close. I realized she meant Dad. "I don't know." I
said after a while.

"Your parents were divorced?"

"Yeah."

"How was that for you, growing up?"

"Hard. Confusing."

She was quiet again. I could tell she was thinking
about her own situation, Frankie.

"What happened with Frankie's dad?"

"I don't want to talk about him."

"OK."

"He was just the little mistake that got the snowball
rolling. But I love Frankie. I really do. I know it's cliché
for young, unwed mothers to wax philosophical about the

choices they've made and how their love for their child made it all worth it. That's only partially true. I hated him when he was born. I was twenty, alone. He was hard to get along with even as an infant. I don't think I slept more than two hours a night the first eighteen months. I was working in a factory in Pittsburgh and living in a trailer out by the highway. It was pink. I left Frankie with a woman a few trailers down who watched kids. Every day at work I thought about him having some kind of accident and at first I was kind of hoping something would happen to him because, 'then I would be free.' I hated myself. Then after a few months I found myself rushing home to make sure he was OK. I stopped being a girl with a kid and became a mother. It doesn't sound like much, but it means everything."

She spoke looking toward the crest of the hill. Her voice was soft, like she was talking to herself.

"That must make me sound like a bad person," she said.

"No. I think I understand what you mean."

"What kind of person admits that they wanted their kid to get hurt?"

"Feeling that way once and admitting it is better than feeling that way and not."

"Maybe." She started walking again and I fell into step beside her. All the hardness she'd had toward me earlier seemed gone, but I looked at her face and she was somewhere else. I wanted to get through to her, have her see me, but I was willing to just walk with her for a while.

We crested the hill and she stopped. "I have to talk to you," she said.

"OK."

"You and me, we're never going to happen."

"Is it about Danny? Are you guys still a thing?"

She waved the thought away. "God, no. That guy was a mistake all the way. I started seeing him not long after I started working at the club. He was fine at first and being a stripper makes you feel like such shit, anyone being nice to you will make you roll over like a puppy that wants its belly rubbed. It didn't take long to see what he really was."

"What's that?"

"A self-important cokehead train wreck."

"Ah."

"What was he like when you were kids?"

"I guess the same and different. I can see what he is now coming from what he was then. But I couldn't see it then. He was my hero, or at least my savior. I was a loser with no friends and he wasn't a loser but still had no friends. We were a perfect match."

"Hard for me to think of him that way," she said.

"I can see that."

She started down the hill and I followed.

"So, why not you and me then?" I said.

"I made a promise. To myself." She didn't look at me.

"What's that?" I moved in front of her so she had to look at me.

"I've been with a few guys. I always start out hoping they'll fit, that they won't go bad, but they always do. And I don't care. I know how that goes. But Frankie takes it hard. He wants someone. He might act tough, but every time one of them goes, he gets further away. I promised myself I wouldn't do that to him anymore."

"I could be different," I said.

"Maybe, but I'm not going to take the chance."

She started walking again. I thought about Stan and all the other guys who'd gone in and out of my life. I understood. I didn't want to, I wanted to be selfish, but I understood. I almost let her go, disappear over the next rise, but I resigned myself to let the day play itself out. I caught up to her. Below us, tucked into the edge of the trees was a little lean-to. She held her hand out to stop me.

"Listen," she said.

I did, but I couldn't hear anything. "What?"

"Can't you hear it? It's him. I knew it."

I listened again and then I heard. Very soft, coming from the lean-to, was a halting rendition of a song I couldn't place. The player was a novice, stopping every couple beats to change chords. There was a thin voice following along, but the words were as indistinct as the melody.

"I bought him that guitar for his birthday. I thought he wasn't playing it. I never heard it in the house. I wanted to wring his neck. I spent a lot of money on that guitar."

We listened until he finished the song or gave it up.

"I don't want him to know we were here," she said.

"We better get back to check on the food anyway."

The turkey still needed some time, so we sat on the couch and watched part of a football game. Dallas looked like they were going to pull it out over the Redskins. I didn't care much about football, but I liked the traditional feel of sitting on the couch on a weekday and watching something usually reserved for the weekend. Anna didn't seem too interested in the game except once, when a Cowboys receiver caught a long pass she said, "Wow." I almost laughed but she didn't seem to notice she'd made a sound, so I kept quiet.

Frankie came home without the guitar. She didn't say a word about it. Frankie looked at me sitting on the couch, rolled his eyes and went straight to his bedroom. Anna was off the couch after him before the bedroom door was fully closed.

"Frankie, don't be rude. John brought stuff for Thanksgiving dinner."

Frankie didn't respond.

"I want you to come out here and apologize."

Still nothing. She stood in front of the door for a minute with her hand on the doorjamb before she came back to the couch. "He'll be out later. He just gets a little shy about new people."

"It's OK," I said. I used to want to die when Mom brought guys home. And now I was that guy. I saw myself through Frankie's eyes and hated me, too. The reality of me was so far away from who I thought I was.

At halftime we took the turkey out and made a small spread on the kitchen table. We didn't talk, moving around each other like we'd worked in that kitchen together for years. We sat down at the table, empty plates in front of us, the food steaming, the good smells all around.

"Should we wait for him?" I said.

"If we do that, we won't eat. He'll come out when he's ready. I can't force him to do anything."

"OK, let's do it," I said and smiled at her.

I was about to reach for the carving knife when she bowed her head and folded her hands in her lap. I was caught in between. I hadn't prayed in years. I didn't want to pray, but I found myself pulling back and folding my hands in my lap. Her lips moved over a silent prayer. I closed my eyes and waited.

After a half a minute, she raised her head and grabbed the dish of potatoes as if there hadn't been a pause. I admired that she prayed and made no excuses, didn't seem uncomfortable about it at all.

The only sounds during the meal were gastronomical. The comfort that was there when we were cooking remained and it was strange to me. I couldn't tell if it was comfort, or indifference on her part. Once our hands touched as we both reached for the rolls she'd made. We each said "Sorry" and I let her take a roll before me. No eye contact, no smile, not intimate, but I didn't feel unwanted or out of place either. The food was good and we ate it fast, each of us carving turkey as we went, filling our plates twice. It was warm in the kitchen. I hadn't felt good like that, close, in a long time. Afterwards we watched the end of the football game while Frankie played punk rock loud in his bedroom. Toward the end of the fourth quarter he came out, got a plate of food, poured ketchup over the turkey and then went back to his room, not once acknowledging us.

"I could give him guitar lessons or something," I said, surprised at myself as I said it. "It's hard to learn if you don't have someone showing you the way at first."

"I got him a book and a video."

"Can he watch the video in that shed?"

"Don't be an asshole."

"I'm not trying to be an asshole, I just want to do something nice for him."

"Why? He doesn't mean anything to you."

She was getting angry. It was hard for me to say why I wanted to help him, but I did.

"Don't get mad," I said. "I remember when I was trying to learn to play and it was hard."

"Don't try and get involved."

"I was just trying to be nice."

"Appreciated, but don't."

"You know, things might be easier for you if you started out trying to trust goodness in people instead of expecting the worse."

"As I recall, I had to drag your drunk, passed-out ass out of the cold before you died of exposure. That's not exactly a first impression you want to remind folks of."

"That wasn't my first impression on you."

She was quiet for a few seconds. "I'm not talking about the club. Your whole thing. You onstage is not you either. You know that. That's what you want people to think you are."

She was right.

Dallas won the game by a touchdown. The station started playing a movie and Anna got up and turned the TV off.

"What do you want to do now?" I asked.

"Shouldn't you go the hospital and check on your dad or something?"

I hadn't thought about Dad for a little while. She saw the guilt in my face. She looked away when I tried to meet her eyes. "Yeah, I guess I should. Can I come back later?"

"No."

"But sometime?"

She looked past me into the kitchen and didn't answer for a minute. "Just don't," she said.

She was asking me to respect her. I said, "OK."

"Thanks for making dinner," she said.

"You shouldn't be so hard on yourself."

"Yeah, well."

I wanted to kiss her on the cheek or something, but she was still looking toward me, not at me. I opened the door.

"Pick up those beer cans before you go."

I plucked the cans out of the brush and stood outside the trailer for a few minutes listening. Nothing. What was she doing in there? Reading? The lights were still on in the living room. Five minutes and no sound at all. I didn't want to leave. Part of me was waiting for her to come to the window and look out. Maybe she would reconsider sending me away. I didn't want to be alone and I didn't want to go back to Dad. She didn't come.

The hospital was quiet. There was a single nurse at the reception desk. Her face was hidden behind a cardboard-and-crepe-paper turkey, the kind that started out flat and then accordioned out to form a full-scale replica of a bird. This particular version had a photo print of a real turkey head. The nurse was reading a paperback romance and was surprised when she saw me peeking over the turkey.

"Oh Jesus," she said. "You scared the jam out of me."

"Sorry."

She folded a corner of the page she was on and put the book face down on the desk. I think she was embarrassed by it. "What can I do for you?"

"I was hoping to see my dad."

She pursed her lips and shook her head. "Oh no, I'm sorry. Visiting hours ended over an hour ago. No one's allowed on the floors."

"I just wanted to see him. He wasn't doing so well. It's a holiday."

She looked from side to side, like there was someone

she didn't want to overhear our conversation. "What's your dad's name? I'll call up and see if I can sneak you in for a minute."

"Ford Martin."

She looked at her computer screen and typed. She knitted her brow and typed again. "Is Martin the first name there?"

"No ma'am."

"Well, I just don't know what's happening. I don't see that we have a Ford Martin registered in the hospital."

"That's not possible. I brought him in here yesterday unconscious. He has cancer."

She tried the name again and shook her head. "No sir, I'm sorry. I don't have your father listed as a patient. I show that he was in Emergency, as you say, but he signed himself out AMA."

"What's that mean?"

"It means he checked himself out against medical advice."

"That doesn't seem possible. He was barely alive yesterday."

"I've seen a lot of impossible. I once saw a guy come in here with a length of rebar through his chest and walk out two hours later."

"Can I talk to the doctor who let him go?"

She looked back to the computer. "He's still on duty. I'll call down and let them know you're on the way."

The doctor confirmed everything that the nurse told me: Dad woke up in the early afternoon, realized where he was, cursed me and anybody who tried to stop him from leaving, and just walked out.

"Did he say where he was going?" I asked.

The doctor shook his head. He was apologetic. They tried to call me at Boulder's but there was no answer. I thanked him, apologized for the trouble and went back to the van. How could he leave? I didn't think Dad could make it back on the hill alone and the only person I knew of that he might call for help was Boulder.

The Kwik Stop was the same as I left it earlier in the day: dark, quiet, closed. I knocked and Boulder didn't come to the door. I put my face to the window. "Boulder," I called out, but nothing. Around back, the old truck was gone.

I sat down on the concrete crossed-legged and tried to think. I couldn't get my mind past the fact that he should still be in the hospital. Any other possibility was beyond what I could process. I sat there for a long time. My heart fluttered in my chest and I went light-headed. It was cold out, dark, but my hands were warm. Traffic rolled by slow, a car at a time, with long intervals between. Who were the people inside those vehicles? On the way to or from Grandma's, groggy with tryptophan, the kids wired on Cool Whip?

A guy alone in a beat down mini-van, the driver's side window held up by duct tape, looked desperate to regain something—his wife, the love of his kids, his job, the ability to operate the taped-shut window and feel the wind on his face as he drove through the mountains? I knew that guy. His face was knit with thought as he rolled by doing the speed limit. He was in his car, but his mind was elsewhere. There were times when I was onstage and I existed without thought, I was simply there, not past, not future, but present. There are whole religions based on trying to get to that place.

I heard Boulder coming back before I saw him. The

great roar came from the direction of town, the sound of
a vehicle that had long ago lost its muffler. I watched the
road, hoping that I would see two silhouettes in the cab, but
when the truck came into view, there was only one. Boulder
guided the truck into the lot, back to the spot where it had
been parked before. I followed and waited for him to get
out. He looked at the ground, like he had to watch his feet
closely on the gravel. I knew he didn't want to meet my eyes.

"Well?" I said.

"He called me from the hospital pay phone, cussing
you. Said he needed me to come get him. He was pissed, but
I could tell it was hard for him to talk. Tell the truth, I was
scared."

I nodded.

"Well, he was cussing and saying he was leaving no
matter what, but I could hear it in his voice that he was in
a lot of pain. I went up there and planned on bringing him
back here, but he wouldn't have it. I helped him in the truck.
We started back this way and he was asking where we were
going. I told him, and the next thing I knew he had the
little .22 pistol I keep in the glove compartment and said if
I didn't drive him back to the hill he'd shoot me. His eyes
were glassy and I don't think he would do anything like that
if he was right in the head, but he wasn't."

"So you took him back up there?"

He shook his head. "This truck couldn't make that
road. We made it back to where he parks that old beater of
his. That's when he really started cussing you. I guess you
took the keys with you."

I reached in my coat pocket. There they were. "So you
left him there?"

"I didn't have a lot of choice. He still had that gun and

he was talking to himself a little. I couldn't make out what he was saying. I've never seen a man so sick still able to move around. I have to say, I was scared of him. He told me to go and I went."

We'd made our way back to the front door of the Kwik Stop. I could see in his face he felt bad. I didn't have any right to be mad at him. What could I expect? I'd have done whatever a half-dead man with a gun told me to do, too.

"You want a cup of coffee?" he said.

I shook my head. "No. I better go look after him."

"I'm real sorry. I wanted to—" He didn't finish the sentence.

"I know you did, Boulder. Don't worry about it."

"He doesn't have much longer. You can see it in his eyes. My mother died of cancer and there was something in her eye just like that, kind of glassy, foggy."

I knew the look he meant. I'd seen it, too. "I better get going."

"You let me know if there's anything I can do."

I shook his hand awkwardly and went to the van. I fought the urge to drive fast through town to get there as soon as I could. I couldn't afford to get stopped for speeding.

I saw him sitting in the passenger's seat, head lolled back and I was sure he was dead. I parked fast and went to the truck. I was relieved when I heard him snoring lightly through the window. I opened the door as quietly as I could and belted him into the seat. I put my hand on his chest to make sure it was rising and falling. I thought he'd wake up when I started the truck, or when we rocked over the first bumps of the dirt road, but he didn't. He didn't stir until we made it to the top of the hill and I cut the engine.

"How are you feeling?" I said.

"Pissed off." His voice was a whisper. I could hear the pain in it.

"Why?"

"Leave me to die in a hospital."

"I didn't leave you to die. I was trying to get you better."

"I'm not getting better."

I got out of the truck and came around to his side. I was mad. Selfish to the end, both him and me. "I wasn't going to just let you die," I said. "People go to the hospital when they're sick."

"I don't want to die in the hospital."

I helped him out of the truck. It was all he could do to move. I practically carried him to the camper. I was scared again. He wasn't going to leave that place still drawing breath. I got him on the bed and fluffed a pillow under his head. Something was going rotten in the garbage so I took it outside and threw it in the foundation of the old cabin. It was dark, but the sky was clear and I stood looking at the stars. In New York I don't know if I ever saw more than the North Star in the whole ten years I was there. Light pollution they called it, from all the streetlights. I never knew I missed it until I stood there that night. The sounds of the hill were all around me, the dry whisper of the knee-high field grass; this is what this hill has sounded like for hundreds, maybe thousands of years. It has sounded this way in its quiet moments no matter what human drama played out across its surface. Every trace of the Martins' time on this land would be gone soon. Did that matter? The stars said no. I wanted another beer, but I'd left the case back at Anna's.

Back in the camper, Dad was asleep. Something stuck out of his pocket: a small envelope with eight pills in it and a prescription for more. I put the pills on the counter and the prescription on the table. I sat at the window and watched the wind move the grass outside. All I could do was sit there and wait.

CHAPTER 10

We spent the next few days on the hill. I went to town for beer, but other than that it was just the two of us. Dad slept mostly, sometimes he seemed better, other times not. I did my best to settle in for a long coexistence. I made us food and puttered around. I started to enjoy it.

I woke sometime before dawn Monday morning from the dream of carrying Dad to the truck. In the dream, he was whispering my name as I carried him. His bones jabbed into me like wire hangers through a trash bag. The trees were on us, talon-branches digging into my neck. I couldn't run fast enough to get away. I opened my eyes and felt pain in my neck from my head lolling to one side. But I still heard the whispering. It took a second to realize Dad really was whispering my name.

"What is it, Dad? Are you OK?" He was trying to sit up in the bed. I went over to help him.

"I'm hurting pretty bad," he said.

"You want to take a couple of these pills?" I took the little envelope off the counter. He nodded. His eyes were closed. There was a milk jug in the little refrigerator that had water in it. There was just enough water left to fill half a glass. I handed him the water and two pills. I wasn't sure if he was supposed to take that many, but I could see the pain in his face. I wanted him to feel better. He choked the pills down.

"Still thirsty," he said.

"There's no more water."

"Down the hill," he said.

"It'll take me over an hour to get to town and back. I

don't want to leave you until you're feeling better."

"No. Spring water, just down the hill. You know the place?"

It was summertime. I was starting high school the next year. It had been a while since I saw Dad. After he and Maggie got married he didn't come around all that much. The every other weekend visits slacked off to once a month, then once every couple of months, then holidays. Finally, all I ever saw of him was a garbage bag full of presents from his side of the family at Christmas and my birthday along with a post-dated check from him. Most of the time we couldn't cash the check. The people at the bank knew he didn't have enough money to back it. One of the detractions of growing up in a town where everyone knew everyone else's business. By the time I left home I had a collection of those checks in my top dresser drawer. I kept them in an old cigar box with a picture of our first dog and a deck of cards my grandfather gave me when I was eight.

That last weekend Dad picked me up on Friday morning. He came after he was sure Mom went to work. The two of them hadn't talked for a long time, not since he stopped paying child support and Mom tried to sue him for it. I didn't know how he convinced her to let me go on the weekend. He lost his visitation rights when he stopped paying. These were facts I allowed myself to forget over the years.

"This neighborhood sure went to shit," Dad said. I just kept looking out the truck window as we came closer to town. I was mad at him. I didn't know why, but I was so angry I was shaking.

"How'd you get Mom to let you take me?" I said. "I

thought you weren't allowed until you paid child support."

"I sent her a check last week."

She hadn't told me that.

"How much?"

"Three hundred."

We drove toward town and I thought about what she might have done with the money.

"How's everything in school?" he said.

"It's summer."

"Yeah, but how's it going? You still getting straight A's?"

"Nope." I got straight A's in grade school, but with junior high came classes like Industrial Arts and upper-level math. Those classes, coupled with my developing vision of myself as a budding rock star and the adoption of the too-cool-for-school demeanor, had created a trough in my GPA. The further it went down, the more I told myself I didn't care. Eventually, I convinced myself I didn't and the transformation from good kid who wanted to please everyone to storm-cloud-browed sloucher was complete.

"You used to do good in school," he said. "What happened?"

"Nothing. Got bored."

We were stopped at a light. He looked at me a long time. He wanted to say something else, but was unwilling to spoil the visit less than five minutes in. We sat through a whole cycle of lights—red, green, yellow, back to red again—him looking at me, me staring out the window. A car came up behind us and tooted when the light turned green again. Dad rolled through and we didn't talk for the rest of the ride.

The cabin was more homey than the last time I was

there. Maggie had hung lacy curtains in the kitchen window and the floor was swept. It was still plywood, but there were a few rag rugs tossed around. There was another chair in the living room—an overstuffed armchair covered in itchy-looking brown fabric. A collection of wedding photos hung crooked on the unpainted drywall. She was all smiles when I came in, cooing over me like a mother hen with "my-how-you've-growns" and other banal BS. She didn't fool me for a second. I knew where we stood. At best, the politeness would last the weekend and there wouldn't be any blow-ups, but I knew already I wanted something to happen. I greeted all her cooing with silence. I stood like a sentry while she half-heartedly fluffed my hair. She tried to hug me and I looped one arm around her shoulder and let it drop.

I spent the rest of the morning out in the fields, just walking. Despite my desire to be sulky and misanthropic I came back at lunch feeling good. I forgot for a while about Maggie and the surly boy I was trying to be. It was hot, but the sun felt good.

My good mood didn't last long. Lunch was on the table when I came back: dippy eggs.

It was well known by anyone who'd ever made me breakfast that I didn't like fried eggs. That was one of the first things Maggie found out about me the first time I stayed with them. I could eat scrambled, Dad's John Wayne eggs because he made them for me, but not fried eggs, which Maggie called "dippy eggs" because she liked to dip her toast in the runny yolks and mop up the yellow shit while forking the egg meat into her face with the other hand. Dippy eggs made me sick. She chewed with her mouth open, another thing I couldn't stand. I smelled the eggs and knew it was on. She wasn't just coming after me;

she was testing Dad, too. Whose side would he come down on?

The two of them were already at the table, arms at their sides, waiting for me.

"I'm not hungry," I said and made for the ladder to the loft.

"Sit down and eat," Dad said. "Maggie went to the trouble to cook lunch and you'll eat it." There was an edge to Dad's voice that hadn't been there in the morning. They'd been fighting while I was out, over me, I guessed. I was glad for that, but Dad's anger made the situation more volatile than I wanted it to be.

It may seem strange that Maggie served breakfast at lunch time, but back then Grandmother had chickens and she butchered a couple pigs every year, so besides deer meat, Dad and Maggie had unfettered access to eggs and pork. The only work Dad had at that time was under-the-table carpentry jobs and a lot of that money went to the VFW; so they ate eggs for breakfast, lunch, and sometimes dinner.

"I don't like fried eggs," I said as I sat down.

"You'll sit and eat what's served." Dad looked at the table. Maggie did, too. I could see the tension in Dad's neck. I wasn't getting out of this without a blowup. I sat down and ate the bacon first. I couldn't look at the eggs. I ate a piece of toast and cut around the edge of one of the eggs and ate the crispy part that tasted OK. I wiped my mouth and put my fork down.

"I'm full," I said.

"Clean your plate," Dad said. Maggie mopped the last of the yolk from her eggs and took her plate to the sink. She stood it the sink, running water, pretending to wash the dishes.

"I don't want to," I said.

"You'll eat them eggs or you won't leave this table." He said it through his teeth. I had to decide how far I wanted to take this. It was him and me now, fighting over something I didn't quite understand. I sat there staring at the eggs for a long time. Finally, I folded them both onto my fork, the yolks bursting and the yellow mucous oozing onto the plate. I got them both in my mouth with fork and hand and I chewed as fast as I could. I gagged and everything almost came out. I put both hands over my mouth and kept chewing. I watched Dad's fists tighten around his fork and knife. I was afraid he might stab me. Why was he doing this? Why had he brought me up there if he only wanted to torture me? I cried as I chewed. The tears fell onto my plate and mixed with the egg yolk. I swallowed. The two of us sat there, the only sound in the room was the water running in the sink.

I let the food settle in my stomach and when I was sure it wasn't coming up I got up and left the cabin. I wanted Dad to follow me out, but he didn't. I walked out in the field toward the far tree line. It was hot. When I disappeared into a swale, invisible from the house, I vomited everything into the brush. I stood there for a long time, spit trailing off my lips, and cried.

I was thirsty after my stomach settled. That's when I remembered the spring. I went to it, crouched to stay out of sight from the cabin. I didn't think I had to hide, but I wanted to. Once I was in the woods, I went down the hill at an angle, back in the direction of the cabin.

The spring water was cold. I held my palms under the trickle and drank until my stomach hurt. The ground surrounding the spring was thick with fern, an undulating carpet of them that stretched out in every direction. I slid myself into the ferns and arranged them over me so I was completely covered. I stayed there for a long time hearing nothing but the trickle of the spring, the trees whispering in the wind, forest sounds.

Footsteps coming down the hill. I stayed still and waited, thinking it could be a deer or a bobcat. The steps came closer and I knew it was Dad, sliding a little as he came down the hill. The footsteps came even with the spring.

He stood on the opposite side of the spring looking down the hill with his arms at his sides. He stood that way for a full minute, not moving. Maybe he was looking for me and maybe not. I could see him clearly between two ferns.

He sat down on one of the stones beside the spring and drank from his palm, then cupped his hand over his face and when he took it away water dripped down his cheeks like he was crying.

I wanted to say something to him then, let him know I was there, but I couldn't. He continued to look at the creek for a while, then stood and looked down at the ferns where I lay. He looked right at my eyes, then he started up the hill. I listened to his footsteps until they faded.

The rest of the weekend went by quiet. We watched a movie on TV that night. Dad took me to the VFW and I shot pool alone. On Sunday, he took me back home. We didn't talk on the way back. He said, "Love you," when I got out of the truck. I didn't respond. I don't know if he ever tried to get me for another weekend. Mom never said one way or another and I didn't ask. I wouldn't have gone anyway.

I stood at the mouth of the spring and watched the water trickle out for a long time, replaying that weekend in my head. I refilled the milk jug as the sun poured orange into the eastern sky. There was no carpet of ferns. No sign of ferns at all.

He was still awake when I got back to the camper. I poured him a glass of water and watched him drink it. He looked better, his eyes clearer. I couldn't see as much pain in his face.

"What?" he said when he finished the water. He noticed me watching him.

"Nothing," I said.

"Don't BS me."

"I was just thinking."

"Yeah?"

"Yeah."

"What about?"

I didn't know what to do. Or, that is, I didn't know if I wanted to get into it. I stayed silent for a long time, thinking about how to get into the conversation. "Why did you make me eat those eggs?" I said finally.

"What eggs?"

"You know what eggs."

He drew in a breath and let it out slow. He didn't look at me. "I thought that's what I was supposed to do."

"Make me eat food I hated until I puked?"

"No."

The sound of us breathing.

"That's it?" I said.

"What do you want me to say?"

"I don't know. Anything. I hated you after that day."

"I know."

"I saw you when you came to the spring. I was laying in the ferns. You put water on your face and it looked like you were crying." I wanted that to hurt him, but it sounded silly coming out of my mouth.

His face was sad. His eyes sunk into his head. He opened his mouth to say something two or three times, but stopped himself. Finally he spoke: "I realized that day that I had fucked everything up so bad that I could never get it right again. I thought I was supposed to be a dad, like my dad was."

We didn't talk again for a long time. I understood him like I hadn't understood before; he didn't know what he was doing. I didn't know what I was doing. No one ever did. It was quiet in the camper. The sun came over the trees and cut through the small window over the sink, a blade of golden light. I was drowsy and wanted to lie down.

He said, "There's a box inside that seat." He pointed to the bench opposite me.

I didn't realize the seat opened and there was storage inside. I lifted the cushion and found a Dingo boot box.

"Bring it here," he said. I carried the box to him and he held it on his lap. He looked like a schoolgirl holding her books while waiting for a bus. "This is everything I ever thought was worth keeping. It's not saying much that a whole life can fit in a box." He ran the palm of his hand over the top, caressing it. He seemed to lose his train of thought but he came back to himself and pushed the box to me. "You can look at it."

I put the box on the table.

"Why didn't you try harder?" I said.

"I did."

"Then why didn't you pay the child support? Why didn't you call me on my birthday? Why weren't you just there?"

"I don't know. It felt like things started going wrong and I couldn't turn it around. I didn't want you to see me fail."

"I didn't care about that. You weren't around."

"I tried."

"That's bullshit." I was so angry all of a sudden I wanted to shake him. I wanted to beat him to death. I saw myself, afraid of the guitar and tapes in the van, looking for any excuse. We were the same. I stood over him and balled my fists. Tears came and I bit the inside of my cheek until I tasted blood. He didn't look up at me.

"Go on and do whatever you're going to do. I can't blame you. Hit me."

I was shaking. I bit my cheek harder, but the tears still came. I pounded the wall over his head, one, two, three times. The wood paneling gave way and my fist rang against the metal skin of the camper. I kept hitting. His white, thin hair moved with my blows like thistle in the wind. I stopped when I saw my blood staining the wall. I stood panting, not looking at him. My hand was swollen already. Would I still be able to play guitar? I flexed the fingers.

"Feel better?" He reached out and tried to take my bleeding hand.

"Fuck you."

He turned my hand over in his. "You better run that hand under some cold water or it'll swell up bad."

I stomped out of the camper like a child and walked back to the spring. My hand started to throb and I thought I might have broken something. I tested the fingers, opening and closing, and everything still worked. I sat by the spring for a while and let the water trickle over my hand. The throb lessened to a pulse, the hand went numb. The water was colder than any water I'd ever felt.

I crawled back up the hill using only the one hand to pull myself up and went to the truck. For a long time, I just sat there and watched the life of the field. A family of deer stepped out of the woods a couple hundred yards away, first the doe and then a fawn, and finally the buck. He was medium-sized, maybe 8-point. They grazed for a while in the open then moved across the clearing and disappeared into the woods on the other side. When they were gone, I put my hand on the key. I didn't start the truck. I wanted a drink. I wanted to drive out of town in any direction and not look back. My hand shook as I held the key. My neck and face itched. I couldn't focus my thoughts. All I could think about was the taste of the first beer, the burn of the whiskey that would follow. I took my hand off the key and drew in a deep breath. I held the breath until my vision got dark around the corners and I saw spots.

I got out of the truck and followed the deer into the forest. I found their trail more easily than I thought I would, disturbances in the leaf bed, a few pellets of shit. I was remembering. I could almost feel the weight of the 30/30 in the crook of my arm. The gun was long gone. On a visit about a year after Dad bought it for me I went to the gun cabinet to take it out and clean it the way he showed me. It wasn't there. I felt kicked in the stomach. It was my gun. Where was it? It took me the whole weekend to ask him about it. He looked at a place above me when he answered.

"I had to sell it to pay some bills. I sold it to Tom Sypolt over on the next hill. Told him I would buy it back off him when I got some money in. He's just holding it for me. They were going to cut off the electric."

I started to cry. "But it was mine," I said.

"I know it and I'm sorry. You'll understand when you're older."

I never saw the gun again.

I wanted these memories to stop. The more that came the more I knew were still to come. Memories I put away a long time ago.

I tracked the deer into the hollow, across the crick and up the next hill. I came to the place where I shot the deer when I was twelve and paused for a minute. It looked both the same and different, smaller, closer, less open. I leaned against the same tree where I leaned before and looked up to where that deer had floated off the ground glowing with morning light. There was no deer now, only the empty space where the deer had been. I lifted my phantom gun and aimed at the spectral deer. I drew a breath and held it and squeezed the ghostly trigger. Boom.

The deer family led me over the next hill, through another hollow. We passed into parts of the forest I'd never seen. I found a cave formed from boulders halfway up a steep rise. I stepped inside, bent over and saw a few tin cans, labels long weathered away. Names written on the wall. I could see the writing, but it was dark and I had no light. The words were faint, old. Some were chiseled in the stone, others written with whatever was available. So many names. So many dates, going back almost a hundred years.

Fear. I'd been wandering the woods in a trance, following the deer, my past, into an unknown place. There was no sound. I could smell the moldering winter forest, the tang of decay. After so many years in the city, silence was more frightening than any sound I could imagine. Anything could happen to me here. I could fall into a ravine, twist an ankle, be mauled by a bear, and there would be no one to know. I was floating with nothing to catch me. I looked at the deer tracks moving farther up the hill. The sun was moving toward the western edge of the sky. How long would it take me to get back? Could I find my way? I had to. The hill crested above me and gave way to an open field. I could keep going and follow the deer, but then what? I was sweating, my breathing shallow. The anxiety took me over and I started on shaky legs back the way I came.

It was almost dusk when I got back to the camper. I looked in on Dad. He was sleeping. I stood outside and let my pulse slow, watching the sun disappear. It was dark inside the camper, cold. It felt as though winter had finally come. There was a bite in the air and it would frost overnight. I lit the halogen lantern and checked the kerosene stove. The reservoir was low. It might not last the night. I watched the dark gather outside the window. I turned the stove as low as it would go and tucked Dad in, pulling the quilts to his chin and securing them under his thin frame. My blood had dried on the wall. I scraped some of it away with my fingernail. I put my hand to Dad's face, clammy and cold. He was so small under the blanket.

I took the boot box off the seat and climbed into the top bunk with the lantern and the box and spent a long few hours going through everything in there. For a while, it was like an invasion of his privacy; an envelope filled with Polaroids of every car he ever owned—the green Nova was there, along with other vehicles I remembered and others I'd never seen, newer, older. The oldest was a '55 Chevy. He talked about that car from time to time when I was young.

I didn't remember that until I saw the picture. There were two pictures, actually. One of him standing at its front fender and the other of the car resting on its side a hundred feet down a hill. For all I knew, it was still there, not five miles away. Dad skidded off the road while racing it and Grandfather made him leave it there. No one ever pulled it out.

The deeper I got into the box, the harder it got to look, but I had to keep going. He had programs from almost every performance I ever gave all the way through high school, when I played Tommy Albright in "Brigadoon" junior year, when I had the solo on an *a capella* version of a Huey Lewis song with the show choir, even the seventh grade spelling bee where I came in second. I never saw him at a single one of these performances. My chest hurt. I wanted to hug him. I wanted to beat on him for never letting me know he'd been there all those times. It would have meant so much to me to know that. I reached the bottom of the box and found the cassette of me singing "(Almost Heaven) Country Roads," recorded on the boardwalk in Ocean City in a little beachside booth. I was proud of that recording, the first time I'd ever recorded anything. I was maybe thirteen. I played it for him sometime later that summer. I hadn't seen him in a long time and he came and we visited in the driveway. He couldn't stay long, he said, but I knew it was because he wasn't allowed to take me anywhere. Mom probably didn't know he was even there. We sat in the truck and he asked simple questions and I gave one-word answers until I found the opportunity to pull out the tape I'd been waiting to show him. I put the tape in the player and he sat and listened with his eyes closed. When the song ended he rewound the tape and played it again. "That sounds professional," he said when it finished playing through the second time. "Can I keep it?" I didn't know how to say no. I only wanted him to hear it, to be proud of me, but I didn't want to let the tape go. I tried to find the word—*no*—but I couldn't. His face was softer than I'd ever seen it.

"OK," I said.

We listened to it over and over again. He kissed me on the cheek, his whiskers rough. He hadn't kissed me since I was a little boy. "You're going to be a big star," he said. "You've got some kind of gift."

At the very bottom of the box was one final Polaroid. This one I took myself. Two men, Dad and his cousin Jimmy, facing one another, each firing old-fashioned musket pistols. My breath went shallow. I hadn't thought of that day for a long time. The day that ended in a duel. It was the Fourth of July, the first time I was ever onstage with a band.

CHAPTER 11

The weekend of the Fourth of July, 1982, was his weekend. The first time a big holiday fell on one of his weekends. I was excited to be there. The best part of the Fourth was always Dad's cookout. We were up at 4:30 in the field about fifty yards from the cabin digging the hole.

"Jimmy says we're getting a big one this year." Dad dug the spade into the ground and the first shovelful of dirt dropped. "We have to make the hole big."

Dad was more animated than I had seen him in a long time. He had a Thermos of coffee with him and drank sips from the little lid that doubled as a cup. He'd chuck his spade into the ground every few minutes and turn to the horizon, watching the light come into the sky, first purple, then blue, then white, the mountains to the east of us in relief against the opening of the day.

We framed the hole about five feet by five and then started digging down. The shovel I used was broken off half way down the handle, the rough edge wrapped with duct tape. I didn't have any gloves and by the time the hole was waist deep the palm of my right hand was raw and blistered. I slacked off and stood blowing on my palm.

"C'mon, John, you gotta work for your supper today."

"My hand hurts," I said.

"Here, let me see."

He turned my hand over in his and inspected the wounds. He spit in my palm and rubbed it in.

"There, that'll get it," he said. "We're almost deep enough here. Go out back and fill the wheelbarrow with brick. Once we get the hole lined we'll get the fire going."

The brick pile was at the edge of the clearing, in a little notch into the woods where Dad put a salt lick a few years before. He hauled the bricks up the hill the summer before, hoping to use them on the cabin, but I guess plans changed. Now they were covered with weeds, surrounded by fern, and I threw a couple rocks into the pile before I got close to scare away the snakes.

The barrow was half full when I heard a noise coming out from the thicket, kind of like a mourning dove song, but too low to be a bird. There was a dense stand of rhododendron just at the edge of the notch where the bricks lay. Beyond the gnarled bush was a flat open space where the trees were not as thick. The morning light filtered gray through the trees and ground fog floated in the swales. I stopped loading bricks and listened but I didn't hear the sound again. Back to work. A few more bricks slammed into the barrow and I heard it again, closer this time, like it was coming from inside the rhododendron. I stayed still and tried to breathe slow, watching the trees. Nothing moved. Then I saw it: in the distance, just far enough away it was hard to be sure I saw it at all, a shock of stark white. I looked harder and saw that the white took shape and became a deer, a small white buck with just the nubbins of antlers on its head. It was maybe thirty or so yards away. I took a step toward it. It heard me and turned its head. It looked right at me with red eyes. We stood there, eyes locked together. I took another step toward the woods and the deer disappeared into the thicket. I ran back to where Dad was finishing the hole.

"You forgot them bricks," Dad said.

"There's something in the woods."

"Oh yeah?"

"Yeah, a white deer."

"No shit?" He'd never cussed in front of me before. "Show me."

"It's gone now."

"Come on."

We went back to the brick pile and I pointed to where the deer had been. There was nothing there.

"What'd it look like?" he said.

"It was all white and had reddish eyes. It was a buck, but it didn't have its antlers all the way yet."

"There's a fella claims he shot an albino buck during bow season a couple years back. Said it was a big one— twelve pointer. Says he got it in the hind end and never caught up with it. I've never seen one. You got a good eye. That's probably luck or something."

We loaded the wheelbarrow and lined the hole with bricks. The sun was out and getting hot.

Jimmy showed up about half an hour later. He drove a ragtop Jeep. It was two-tone brown and when I was really little I loved to climb on the spare tire that hung from the back and jump off yelling, "Jimmy Calhoun!" Jimmy was one of those guys who made you laugh all the time. He was missing a couple teeth in the front and his hair was long and always greasy, but he used to play football with Dad in high school and you could see the quarterback frame underneath the beer belly that hung over his belt. In the summer, he wore cut off jean shorts and a western shirt with the sleeves torn off, the front unbuttoned.

We heard him coming up the hill long before we could see him. He drove that Jeep hard, coming up the back road, the older road that was almost washed out in a few places. It was the only road Jimmy would take. The new road up the front of the hill was "too sissy" he said.

He gunned the Jeep out of the forest and looped across the field, taking a wide turn and then sped right for us, bouncing over the little rises in the landscape. Dad watched him come. I tensed up and he cupped my neck in his hand.

"Don't move. Just let him come."

He must have been going over forty when he reached us. He pulled the wheel to the left and the Jeep banked hard, going up on two wheels for a second before settling back to the earth. He slammed the brakes and spun around so he was facing back the way he came. The canvas door on the driver's side flew open and he rebel yelled at us as he jumped high off the running board and landed in the hole we'd dug for the pig.

"Out of the goddamn frying pan into the fire. Please don't eat me." He flapped his arms all over his body like he was trying to put out the fire.

"Stop being a sonofabitch."

"Yessir, General Martin, sir." He gave Dad a "Heil Hitler" salute and goose-stepped out of the hole. We filled it with wood, dumped a lawnmower can's worth of gas on it and started the burn. The flames rose high above our head before they died down and smoldered.

The heat started to come into the day, thick and heavy. Jimmy went back to the Jeep and opened the gate. Inside, the pig he'd brought was so big it couldn't lay flat.

"Where you get that monster?" Dad said.

"I have to plead the fifth on that one, my friend."

"Lindamood?"

Jimmy put his fingers to his lips and turned them like he was turning a key. He slipped the pretend key into the watch pocket of his jean shorts and smiled.

"Well, shit," Dad said. "Let's get this thing wrapped and in the hole before all hell breaks loose."

"Hold on, Ford. First things first. I haven't had my breakfast. Why don't you come over here and help me get my date out of the Jeep."

The keg was belted into the passenger seat. Jimmy and Dad lifted it out and rolled it toward the cabin.

"John-boy," Jimmy called back to me, "get that ice out of the back seat."

I did as I was told and then helped him get the keg into an old oil barrel and dump the ice in. Dad got the pig ready, wrapping it first in foil and then in wet burlap. We rolled the pig in and shoveled the dirt over it.

"Remember," Jimmy said, "Nobody eats until that pig comes out of the ground."

Dad nodded. I was worried. We hadn't had breakfast yet and I was hungry.

"Dad, I don't think I can make it that long."

"Jimmy meant the grownups. We'll get you something directly."

"Here's your breakfast, General." Jimmy handed Dad a plastic cup and the two of them toasted the sun just over the tree line.

The rest of the crowd started showing up by mid-morning. Some came with tents and set them up in the fields and others brought sleeping bags and blankets and laid them out beside their vehicles. By noon a band had set up in the shadows of the cabin. I watched them standing off to the side, excited when the guitar player first drew a chord out of his guitar.

It got hotter and hotter as the sun rose over the trees

toward its highest perch in the sky. People started drinking, playing horseshoes. There were other kids, too, but I didn't know any of them. They went to school out in the county and I went to the city school. They ran in packs through the tall field grass, chasing each other with sticks, tackling one another, boys and girls alike. Part of me wanted to be with them, but I stayed away, fearing the same treatment the neighborhood kids gave me. I watched the band set up. I'd seen bands on TV, but I'd never seen one up close.

By noon it was hot. A lot of the women took off their shirts and ran around in bikini tops or their bras; the men peeled off their shirts, revealing torsos so white they hurt my eyes to look at them in the sunlight. Their arms were dark brown or red to where a T-shirt sleeve would hit so they looked kinda like a negative image running through the field catching a Frisbee or working their elbows with beer cup in hand.

The women weren't taking part in the "no eating until the pig's cooked" rule, but they were drinking right along with the guys. When the band started playing, most of the adults slammed themselves together in a furious, two-stepping knot in the grassless cabin dooryard. It hadn't rained in a while and the dust cloud rose slowly around them and the players until the haze and the sun made the group seem to glow from where I sat on a stack of cinderblock in the shade cast by the cabin itself. The band played mostly country stuff, with some old rock thrown in. The lead guitarist was good and I remember him turning to the rest of the group all the time, waving the neck of the guitar at them, pulling them back together when the rhythm fell apart.

After about an hour they took a break. Everyone

was dripping sweat. The ground was wet with beer and perspiration. Most of the dancers wandered into the field and lay down or stumbled to the keg to get more beer. The band stayed with their instruments and drank and smoked, sitting on their amps, talking amongst themselves. They were separate from the rest of us, even though one of them was my second cousin and the others all went to school with Dad. They were a club. There seemed to be something unspoken between them, the way they caught each other's eye and grinned, like they were in on a private joke. That's the first time I remember noticing that about musicians. I was jealous of them.

Dad came around the back of the cabin and talked for a minute with the guitar player. He nodded a couple times and then they looked my way. Dad waved me over.

"You want to sing a song with these guys?" he said.

I didn't know what to say. I was scared. The answer was "yes" and "no" all at once.

"I don't know any songs," I said.

"Yeah you do."

I looked at the ground.

"You know 'Blue Suede Shoes,' Frank?" Dad said.

"Does the Pope piss in the woods?"

Dad knelt down to look me in the eye. "You wanna sing that one?"

I don't know how long I waited to answer. It felt like everyone in the field was looking at me. "I don't know if I know it all," I said.

"I've heard you do it with the tape. You don't have to if you don't want to."

I wanted to. It took me a second to work up the guts to say, "All right."

Frank said, "If you get stuck I'll come in with you. Just watch me for when to start."

Frank moved to the microphone. "Hey everybody," he said, "Ford's boy John's gonna sing one for you." A few people clapped. "He's got one of the best singing voices I've ever heard. Why don't you all come on down and yell for him."

They rose out of the grass like the living dead and marched toward the cabin again. Frank took the mic from its clip and handed it to me. It was heavier than I thought it would be, like a good, old Matchbox car, and cold even in the afternoon heat. I put the mic to my mouth and smelled spit.

"Blue Suede in G," Frank said to the band. He bent down to my ear and said, "Tear it up," then he counted off.

In the center of the group, with all the instruments pounding into my back, there was a power I never felt before. There were no more people, there was no more field, only the sound. My voice came back at me from the little monitor speaker on the ground and I heard myself sing for the first time. I don't remember anything from the first moment I opened my mouth until there was an instrument break and Frank took a long solo. The song flowed and I was there with it, lost and found all at once. When he finished his solo he winked at me and I went through the first verse again. I knew every word without thinking. The song just came to me. The band crashed together to the end.

I walked away from the band light-headed, ears ringing and in love. Everyone who'd been dancing collapsed around me and shook me by the biceps, ruffled my hair, one woman kissed me on the mouth. It was a sloppy kiss that smelled like spit and beer. Dad came over and shook my hand. He didn't say anything. His lips were a tight, straight line and his eyes were soft. We looked at each other for a minute and I felt close to him. I wandered into the field feeling drunk.

It takes almost twelve hours at least to cook a pig in the ground. By that math, at five o'clock that Fourth of July, when everything went bad, we had another hour to go before the food might have saved us.

Jimmy was drinking like it was his job. He'd start at the keg, fill up, drink a little, top it off, then make his circuit around the field, flirting with the single girls, sipping from flasks, tossing the football with the high school kids who gathered around a Bronco at the back end of the field by the old cattle gate. I realize now they were back there away from the crowd so they could smoke pot. That was hippy shit and Dad hated anything that was hippy shit.

Jimmy was more of a modern dude though. He was willing to get fucked up by any means available and that Sunday he went around the field sampling a little of everything available. At around three, I had to go to the bathroom so I went back to the outhouse. Jimmy was there puking into the brush twenty feet away. He heard me coming and stood up, wiping his mouth with his shirttail.

"Hey Singer," he said, "had to make room for more." He tripped over a root and fell into me. "Who put that there?"

The next time I saw him he was back at the keg in a chugging contest with his cousin, Chub. Chub looked like his name. There was a cheesy quality to him, like he was made of cheese, or sweated cheese. He stank like sweat and mildew and you could grease a pan with the run-off from his hair. He went everywhere Jimmy went. His one redeeming quality was his ability to drink anything, as much he could get down, and be steady as Moses behind the wheel.

Jimmy won the chugging contest and took off at a sprint past the cabin to the road. He ran for another hundred yards or so and stopped, bending over again to throw up in the short grass between the tire ruts.

He stayed bent over for a few minutes then came running back up the road. He leapt in the air when he got to the keg and grabbed the tap, pouring beer directly down his throat.

"You know what day it is, sonsabitches?" He jumped onto the tailgate of Dad's truck and threw his arm around Dad's shoulders. "It's fucking Independence Day. Fucking American Revolution. George Washington was a badass. You know what those fuckers did back then? They had duels. You remember that guy Hamilton? He was the vice president or something. Got killed in a duel. He fought with Washington. That's the way to go."

Some of the guys around the truck grunted soft agreement but feet started to shuffle.

"You ever been in a duel, Ford?"

"Can't say I have."

"You wanna?"

"Settle down, Jimmy."

"I got my muzzle loaders in the Jeep. We could just load the powder and wadding and do it for fun."

"Jimmy."

"What are you, yellow?"

The other guys around the keg moved away from them a little. I could tell Dad was getting mad. He had the same look on his face he did when him and Mom fought and he was trying not to yell—flat, expressionless, slack.

"Just stop it," he said. "I got my boy here."

"Chicken shit. What kind of example are you setting for young Singer there?" Jimmy laughed and Chub laughed along with him, louder than he needed to. A few of the other guys chuckled.

"You're a sonofabitch." Dad moved toward the Jeep.

Jimmy hopped off the tailgate and dug into the backseat of the Jeep. He came out with a wood case a little smaller than a briefcase. He busied himself with the guns, pouring in powder then biting off wadding and ramrodding them into the barrels. Dad watched, still expressionless. He looked at me once and he seemed sad. Jimmy finished with the guns and came over to Dad. He had a greasy rag in his hand.

"I challenge you, sir," he said and slapped Dad with the rag. Dad didn't do anything at first. He sat there frozen. Jimmy swung the rag again and Dad caught his arm and pushed him down in the dirt.

"No need to be nasty," Jimmy said.

"Fuck yourself."

The two of them walked to the road, each holding a gun. Everyone kept back, and a line formed on each side of the dirt track.

"Shoot him down, Ford," someone called out. Jimmy flipped him off.

"Ten paces, turn and shoot," he said. Dad nodded.

"Shit, I forgot." Jimmy ran back to the Jeep and came back with a Polaroid camera. He handed it to me.

"When we hit ten, shoot a picture for us, young Singer."

The two of them lined up back-to-back and Jimmy

said, "Ready? Go," and stepped off the first of the ten steps, calling out each step as he went. I raised the camera to my eye. I thought someone would stop them, but "eight, nine, ten," they turned and I snapped the picture. The guns roared like cannons, which I guess they kind of were. There was a lot of smoke. Before it cleared I could hear Jimmy screaming.

"Mother of fuck." His voice broke and he moaned, bawling like a branded calf.

I remember the smoke, the way it floated between them. I watched it for a long time, blue and thick, until it drifted into the haze of the white sky.

The wadding from Dad's gun had hit Jimmy in the shoulder and spun him around. He landed in a tire rut where he stayed and whimpered and screamed. He tried to move his arm. The pain was too much and he threw up in the dust. "You didn't take big enough steps," he said. "You were too close. You fucking did it on purpose."

"You're a drunk idiot," Dad said. Jimmy had missed him completely.

"Fuck you."

Chub helped Jimmy up by his other arm. Jimmy threw his gun at Dad. It landed in the dirt at his feet. He dropped the other gun next to the one Jimmy had thrown. The crowd parted as Chub helped Jimmy to the Jeep. Dad came over to me.

He said, "Jimmy gets too drunk sometimes."

"I thought you guys were friends."

"We are and we aren't. Things are different when you get older."

He left me standing by the road still holding the camera. In all the craziness, I hadn't even taken the picture out of the slot. I pulled it free and looked at the developed photo, which caught the two men just after the pistols had fired, Dad leaning back, blue smoke puffed out of his barrel and Jimmy in the left of the frame spinning after the wadding hit his shoulder. It was a frightening and exciting picture. I almost ran to show Dad, but stopped myself. I cupped the picture in my hand and looked at it. It was like they were dancing and Dad had twirled Jimmy and then let go. There was something beautiful about it, Dad firm, planted in the ground and Jimmy, twisting out of control. I put the picture in my front pocket and watched the people around me get back into the swing of the day.

The party was quieter after that. Chub drove Jimmy to the emergency room and Dad and a couple other guys dug the pig out of the ground. Everyone ate.

At dusk the bats came out. They swooped out of the trees, over the field, diving toward the ground, scaring all the kids. Somebody's dad showed us that if you threw a stick up in the air, the bats would fly at it, thinking it was prey. There were maybe twenty or thirty of them out there and ten of us kids throwing sticks up. The bats swarmed at them. I could hear their wings flapping, not rustling like birds, but furry skin on skin. After a while they went away again, the fires died down and the clearing got quiet. I could hear people, but the moon wasn't out, so I couldn't see them. I went to sleep that night with the Polaroid inside my pillowcase. I meant to take it out the next morning but I forgot.

CHAPTER 12

"You remember this?" I asked Dad in the morning. I helped him sit up and fed him another couple pills, the last two. I'd have to go into town soon to get more. I didn't want to leave him. He looked smaller still there among the quilts, like he was fading away. The kerosene had run out in the heater. There were only two cans of chili left.

He looked at the picture. "That wasn't one of my better days."

"I thought you did OK."

He shook his head. "He was trying to embarrass me and I couldn't let him do it. He always liked that you idolized him. He never had anyone else like him like that, except Chub."

"Whatever happened to Jimmy?"

"He died. Must have been ten, eleven years ago. Got drunk and drove his Jeep off a ridge into a railroad cut."

I was surprised, but I don't know why. It made sense that he would die like that, but I expected him to still be perched on a barstool somewhere or driving the Jeep breakneck through the hollow.

Dad said, "I'm just surprised it didn't happen sooner. He always pushed it too hard, especially after high school."

"Why?"

"He had to stop playing football. Tore something up in his knee. He was good. I mean, really good. Had a scholarship to go to college. He went and his knee wouldn't hold up so he tried to join the Army with me. They wouldn't take him. By the time I came back, he was different. He let his hair grow and started drinking and drugging. It was a shame."

He was out of breath from talking, his voice a hoarse whisper. I poured him some more water.

We were quiet again. I thought he'd gone back to sleep, but after a few minutes he said, "How you doing?"

"I'm all right."

"I mean after yesterday."

"I don't know."

There was no other sound in the camper but his breathing.

"If I was you, I would have beat me silly and not the wall," he said.

"Well, you're not me." I flexed my fingers. The hand had swollen up in the night. "Let's just forget it."

"You ought to see a doctor. That doesn't look right."

"People in glass houses," I said.

He said, "Uh-huh," and was quiet for a minute. He drew another breath to talk and started coughing. His coughing was weaker than it had been before. Nothing came up. He was drowning in himself.

I opened a can of chili and ate it cold. I made a list in my head of the things I needed to get in town.

"Hey," he said, "don't get all quiet on me. I still got a little left in the tank." He shifted on the bed, trying to lift himself but he made a small sound, almost a squeak and couldn't raise up. I helped him. He was half sitting, half laying and his face was so pale, almost translucent.

"You still in pain?" I asked.

"Yeah."

"Bad?"

"Yeah."

"If you're gonna be all right for a little while I could go

out and get that prescription filled. I gave you the last two pills a while ago."

He nodded. "I'm gonna close my eyes for a minute."

The sun was out, but it was still cold. Frost crunched under my boots. I needed to get kerosene for the heater. I looked to the spot where I'd seen the family of deer in the field. It was empty.

Monday morning in town looked a whole lot like any of the other days I'd seen thus far. A few trucks on the road, but there was no bustle of folks on their way to work after the long weekend. The long-closed stores were still closed. The moldering houses too close to the road still loomed, collecting coal dust and grime. The pharmacy was still in the same place, just across the street from the bank. I used to buy comic books in there. I walked in expecting to see the wire racks with Spider-Man and The X-Men still just inside the door but the place had changed. The front part of the store was a kind of junk shop with old rusted signs from stores that had closed when I was a boy—Teet's Farm Service, Miller's Meat. There was the old Sunoco sign from Howdy's station. How long had it been closed? I wondered where I could get the kerosene. I thought about buying the sign until I saw the price tag read $50.

"Can I help you?"

I turned from the signs to see the very same woman who always ran the place. She was small and thin, with curly hair that had been charcoal black when she was younger, but now she was much older and her hair was mostly white.

"That's a lot of money for an old sign," I said.

"It's a collector's piece."

"It's still kind of crusty."

"There are a lot of people who collect old signage. It's

priced within a reasonable window."

The words came out of her mouth like she was reading from a script. She was trying to make the transition the rest of the town hadn't made yet, from living community with a future to a diorama of itself, a curio shop, a snow globe. She was getting angry with me. I'd touched a nerve.

"Do you still fill prescriptions here?" I said.

"We do."

"I need to fill this for my Dad." I handed her the prescription and she walked me to the back of the store where she went through a small half door into the pharmacy work area and slipped on a white lab coat.

"Does your father have an account on file with us?"

"I'm not sure."

She took out a small box of note cards, balanced a pair of reading glasses on her nose, and thumbed through. She found a card, yellow with age, and pulled it out.

"Yes," she said, "we do have your father on file. He hasn't filled a prescription with us for some time. Is this contact information still accurate?"

"I doubt it."

She took out a pen. "Please give me his current address so I can update the file."

"He doesn't really have an address."

"Where does he live?"

"That's hard to explain."

She pursed her lips and glowered at me over the glasses. She thought I was screwing with her. "I don't think I can fill the prescription without up-to-date information."

"Look," I said. "I can't really explain. My Dad's had a tough time and he's really sick with cancer. He needs those pills. He's in a lot of pain."

She looked at the card again. "Your grandmother was Ida Martin."

I nodded. I hadn't heard her name in a long time.

"She was ahead of me in school." She looked at the card and the prescription again, then turned and went to into the back. She came back with the pills. I took out my wallet.

"That's seven dollars."

I hesitated. "Why so little?"

"Your father has VA benefits. They have a very reasonable co-pay."

I handed her my credit card and she pursed her lips again. She didn't want to charge so little. It probably cost her money. She ran the card and brought back the slip for me to sign and the pills inside a slim white bag. I thanked her and she nodded. She didn't say she hoped he got better or anything else. She just nodded. She knew what was in store for the recipient of that particular prescription.

I was on the way to the van when I was tackled from behind. Fists pounded into my kidneys.

"What the fuck," I said and squirmed around to face my attacker. I got my arms over my face just in time to block Dan Field's roundhouse right. While he reloaded, I took my chance and kneed him in the crotch. He doubled over and rolled off me.

"Jesus, man," I said. "What the hell's wrong with you?"

"Don't act innocent. You always acted innocent. I know what you're doing." He was up on one knee, sucking air.

"Why don't you tell me so we can both be in on it."

"I didn't say you could fuck her."

He was talking about Anna.

"I'm not doing anything with her. And you're not either. She told me you two were done."

"Fuck no."

"Well, that's not what she says, and anyway, she doesn't want me."

"I saw you leaving her place."

"She saved me from hypothermia. I made her and Frankie dinner to repay her."

"You're a fucking liar." He came at me like a lineman out of a three-point stance. I side-stepped and he ran headfirst into the bumper of a Buick. And then, without really thinking, I was on him. I couldn't punch because of my hand, so I kicked him once, twice, three times. He curled up like a potato bug and I kept kicking. I always hated him. I knew that now. I always hated that he was cooler than me. I always hated that he was the only friend I had. It all came out there. I fell to my knees and beat on him with my forearms. But I wasn't doing any damage. He had himself protected. The blacktop beside the Buick was broken into loose pieces the size of dinner plates. I grabbed a piece of it and held it high over my head.

And then I stopped.

I kept the blacktop above my head for a few moments before I lowered it.

"I'm done," I said. I stood over him. "Just leave her alone. She's trying to raise her kid. Don't fuck with her."

He didn't answer. I waited until my breathing slowed. He got up and looked at me.

"You got stronger than you used to be," he said.

I laughed.

As fierce as his anger had been moments before, he was smiling like we were old buddies again. "You really not doing anything with her?"

I shook my head.

"You staying in town?"

"I don't know."

"Well, come out and see me. I heard what happened at the club. You're back in." He slapped me on the shoulder, draped his arm around me, and squeezed.

"You wanna get something to eat?" he said.

"I gotta get back."

"Where are you staying?"

"With my dad."

"No shit, really?"

"Yeah. He's pretty sick."

"Damn. Sorry." He squeezed my arm and tried to make eye contact.

"You know where to find me," he said and punched me lightly on the shoulder. "You're a crazy sonofabitch." He walked away.

I checked the package of pills in my pocket. Still intact. Across the street was the bank. I thought about my empty wallet. Time to see if there was anything in there waiting for me.

Inside, the bank was much the same. The furniture was different from when I was last there, but still out of date. The brass-railed teller windows hadn't changed. I went to the small customer service desk and told the woman sitting there that I wanted to talk to someone about my mother's estate.

She said, "Oh, I'm so sorry," and patted me on the hand. She had a genuine look of sadness in her eyes at what she thought was a recent loss and I didn't have the heart to tell her she was mistaken. She guided me to the waiting area.

A few minutes later a man came and collected me. He was young, maybe twenty-four and I felt a little like my grandmother, as I distrusted his ability to successfully complete my banking at such a young age. He sat me in front of his desk and went through the same prepared spiel designed for grieving customers. I explained that Mom had been dead for a while and his shoulders slumped a little like he was disappointed, either that he'd gone through the speech for nothing or that he didn't get to finish the whole act. I didn't like him. He sucked at his teeth and ran his tongue over them again and again. His teeth were very white, unnaturally white. He excused himself and went to find her files. When he came back he asked me to show him some ID. I did. Satisfied that I was who I claimed to be he opened the folder.

"Yes, I see here that your mother's will directed that all of her assets should be sold, debts paid, and then the remaining funds were signed over to her attorney who was to then distribute the money to charity."

"Charity?"

"That's correct."

"How much money?"

"Thirty-one thousand dollars."

I took a few seconds to let the number settle. My mind went to the tapes in the van, the empty wallet in my pocket.

"What was the charity?" I said.

"That's not indicated. You'd have to take it up with the attorney who oversaw your mother's estate, Mr. Barill." The banker tried to look at his watch discretely, half-hiding his arm under his desk, but he wanted me to know that if

I wasn't going to dump any coin in his coffers then he was ready to move on with his day. I thanked him for his time and wandered out of the bank a little stunned. Until he said thirty-one thousand dollars, I hadn't admitted that I was hoping there would be some money for me. My face flushed. My eyes grew hot and tears welled. I felt betrayed. I stood on the sidewalk and watched the traffic roll through town.

I found Barill's law office address in the phone book. He was down on Front Street in an office above the historical society. It was the only building that was kept up, an old federal-style two story, pillars fresh-painted white, brickwork clean. The front door was open so I went in and climbed the stairs to the second floor. His name was stenciled on a pebbled glass door. It was like I'd stepped back in time. I tried the door but it was locked. I knocked and there was no answer. I tried again louder but nothing. I heard movement in the office across the hall. The door opened and a small older woman with skin like a bald dog poked her head out.

"He's not in there. You can stop banging."

"Do you know when he'll be in?"

"Not today. Maybe not this week. It depends. It's the first day of buck season. Everybody's out in the woods today."

"But I need to talk with Mr. Barill."

"I guess you'll have to try back."

I thanked her and she closed her door without saying anything else. I always remembered the people of my hometown as friendly and willing to help, but the longer I'd been back, the more they struck me as suspicious and private. Were they always like that or had they changed? Or had I? I knocked on her door. It took a while for her to come back.

"Yes?" she said. She only opened the door six-inches.

"I need to buy some kerosene. Where's the closest place?"

"The Exxon out by the Maryland border. All the other places in town stopped selling gas since that place went in. Sucked up all the business."

She closed the door before I could thank her.

I was hungry again. I went back to the van and ate a granola bar, but I wanted to find some real food soon.

The drive to the Exxon was stunning. Every car that passed, every truck, was laden with an animal. A deer lashed over the fender of a Grand Am, a head lolling out of the back of a Subaru wagon, two bucks tied to the roof rack of a Hyundai SUV, pickups with gun racks sporting one or two firearms apiece. Cars and trucks were empty along the side of the road stationed at the edge of every copse of trees. I don't know how many times I saw this as a boy and it never fazed me. Now after so many years in the city it was like deer Armageddon. I found myself stuck in a traffic jam as I approached Boulder's place. He was still the game check-in spot and there was a line of cars waiting. It took ten minutes to get past. I saw Boulder standing in the lot, looking over the kills, checking the hunting licenses. I'd never seen so many dead animals in one place. Some hunters were smiling, proud, others seemingly in shock.

I drove on to the border, bought the kerosene, and then went on to the Food Lion. On the way I'd passed the road to The Farm and I thought about Anna. I wanted to see her but I respected what she said about Frankie. I admired her sacrifice. Was not being with me really a sacrifice? I didn't want to be Stan and no matter how hard I tried I probably would be.

The groceries and the kerosene took an $80 chunk out of my credit card. I came to The Farm road again on the way back and saw that the game-checking line coming back into town was half a mile long. I couldn't sit in that line. I didn't have anything frozen in the grocery bags, nothing perishable, but an hour with a dead deer sticking its tongue out at me from the back of a Dodge Omni would send me over the edge. I took the turn without letting myself think about how Anna might react to my coming. I really wanted to see her.

Her truck wasn't parked in front of the trailer. I pulled the van in beside her spot and let the engine idle. I watched the windows. She wouldn't be in there, the truck was gone. The girl I'd watched before came out to tend the chickens again. She waved to me and I waved back. I saw Frankie's face in the living room window. He saw me see him and disappeared. Did I want to talk to him? Should I?

I got out of the van and knocked on the screen door. He didn't come. There was a distant thump of music. I knocked again and nothing. I had to knock with my left hand. The right had become swollen and discolored. Maybe Dad was right. I should see a doctor about it. And pay for that with what?

"Frankie," I called. "Open up. I know you're in there." The music grew louder. I started to get mad. I kicked the bottom of the door frame three times. Each blow made a black scuff mark on the aluminum. The music dialed down. Footsteps pounded through the trailer and the door opened a crack.

"Jesus-fucking-Christ, dude. You're gonna knock the place down. What the fuck do you want?"

"I'm looking for your mom."

"She's not fucking here." He opened his eyes wide and gestured toward the empty parking space.

"Yeah, OK. Well, can I hang out until she gets back?"

"Why?"

"I don't know. Because I want to. Maybe you and me could hang out."

"I don't want to hang out with you. What are you, some kind of fag?"

I don't know why I wanted to hang out with him, but I did. I knew what it was like to be alone like he was. Not easy. Maybe I could help him. No one had called me a fag since junior high. It still stung.

"I'm not a fag," I said.

"Well, I don't want to hang out. I just want to be left alone. I'm tired of you guys who want to fuck my mom acting all nice and trying to be my friend. It's all a scam. You just want to get in her pants and think that if you're buddies with me that'll get you in. Well, I say fuck you."

I should have just turned and left. I don't know why I didn't. I felt real tenderness toward him and that surprised me. I didn't say anything for a few seconds. I looked at my boot marks on the door frame.

"You're not fooling anybody with your black clothes and acting all hard," I said. "I know you. I used to be you. You could be me. Just think of me as the ghost of fucked up Christmas future."

I expected the door to close. That's what I would have done when I was his age. I didn't look at him. I just stood there. He let the door swing open.

He said, "If you try to touch me, I'll beat you to death."

I sat down on the couch and he went back into his bedroom. The music shut off. He came back into the room and sat in the armchair across from me. He lowered his head and glared at me. It was a pose and it wasn't working, but he was trying. It was over-hot in the trailer, the way trailers always are. Sweat popped on my brow, but I didn't release his gaze.

"You're not going to scare me with that look," I said.

"I'm not trying to scare you."

"Yes you are."

"Fuck if you know what I'm trying to do."

"Stop saying fuck so much. It loses its potency with repeated use."

"Fuck you."

"Look at me if you want to look at me, but stop with the death metal glare. It's getting comical."

He looked away. I couldn't tell if he was angry or crying. When he turned back to me his face had changed. Years had come off it and he looked like the thirteen-year-old boy he was—open-faced, scared, alone.

"What do you want to talk about?" he said.

"I have no idea."

"I don't want to just sit here."

"What do you want to talk about?"

"I dunno." He chewed at a hangnail on his index finger. It was already red and looked painful but he chewed and seemed to lose himself in it. His eyes went somewhere far away. I thought about how I used to pick my nose and eat the boogers. I did that until I was about his age. A girl I liked in school saw me do it in gym class and told her friends and by the time the school day was over I became "booger-eater," a nickname that stuck for the rest of that quarter. I can still hear the chorus of girls—many of whom I was secretly in love with—"*booger-eater, booger-eater, booger-eater.*" Then came the summer and I did my best over the whole break to cure myself of the habit. When school started again I braced myself for the nickname. I feared I was going to be "booger-eater" for the rest of my life. But sometimes kids have a short memory for those things, I guess, and the name never came back. I never ate my boogers in school again either.

"You got any games or anything?" I said.

"Like board games?"

"Not necessarily. Like video games."

"N-64."

We played Mario Kart for about a half hour. He beat the crap out of me in every race and I saw him relax, become the loose-limbed kid he should have been. He was letting me in, but I'd be out of his life again soon enough. I knew that. The guilt made my chest feel tight. After the fourth race I cried uncle and got us glasses of Coke from the refrigerator.

"You're a professional musician?" He said. He chewed on his finger some more and wiped it on his jeans.

"Kind of. I almost was."

"What does that mean?"

"I don't know."

"Whatever." His scowl came back. He knew I was bullshitting him.

I said, "I mean, I never really made a living at it. I got a record deal and some money from that, but I pissed most of that away and my record never came out."

"But you still do it, right? You still play?"

"Not really."

"Why not?"

"It's hard to say. I lost touch with it. I don't know if I'd have the strength to try to get it back. I don't know if I could stand to fail again."

"But you didn't fail."

"How so?"

"You got a record deal. You made a CD."

"Yeah, but nobody ever heard it."

He shrugged. I almost told him he'd understand when he was older, but I didn't. I'd had that line used on me enough times. And I wasn't sure it was true.

"Play me something," he said.

"Naw. I don't think I know anything you'd like."

"I don't care. I just want to hear you do something. Mom said you were really good."

"She did?" I wanted to hear more about what she thought of me.

"Yeah."

"What else did she say?"

He shrugged again. "Not much. She doesn't really talk to me about stuff. I asked when I saw your guitar case the other day."

"I like your mom," I said.

"I know."

"You think she likes me?"

"Fuck if I know. She's got problems."

"Don't we all," I said. We laughed. "I don't think I can play," I said. "I messed up my hand."

"Don't be a pussy."

I went out to the van and got my guitar. He sat on the love seat beside my left hand and watched my fingers the whole time I played. I gave him something fast, or at least mid-tempo, which is about as fast as I get. When I finished he nodded.

"That was cool," he said. "I hate that kind of music, but you're good."

I was glad he was impressed.

"How did you learn to play?" he asked.

"I taught myself. I got some books, Beatles mostly, and learned how to play out of those. I sat for hours in my bedroom when I was your age and tried to figure out songs I liked."

"That's cool."

"Now it's your turn," I said.

"No way."

"Come on. I played. It's only fair."

"I suck, dude. I don't even have a guitar."

"Yeah you do. Your mom told me she bought you one."

"I left it outside and it got messed up." He let his shoulders slump and his voice dropped a notch.

"Why'd you do that?"

"I didn't want anyone to hear me."

"Who's chickenshit now?" I held my guitar out to him. He looked at it.

"I don't want to," he said.

"Yeah you do. I bet you're pretty good. Or are you too chicken to show me?"

He said, "Fuck you, man," but smiled when he said it. He took the guitar and plucked at it unsure of himself for a few seconds, but then he formed a D chord and started strumming something slow. A rhythm took shape, a little melody. He ran through a simple set of changes: D/Em/C.

The song was lighter than I expected. I thought he was just going to play the chords. He went through the changes four times, but the fifth time around he started singing. It was hard to make out the words, but he had a soft tenor voice that floated out of him. He was unsure of how to use it, but it was lovely. The only words I could make out were "suffer in silence." When he was done I clapped my hands softly.

"That was awesome," I said. "You're really good."

He looked at his lap, but I could see he was smiling. "Thanks," he said.

"You wrote that?"

"Yeah."

"That's good. I couldn't do that when I was your age."

"Thanks." He handed the guitar back to me.

We were quiet for a few seconds. I wasn't sure what to do. I was out of tricks, but I liked being there. I wanted to be his friend, but I knew there was a no chance. Anna was right.

The groceries in the car, the prescription, Dad alone in the camper came back to me. "I better get going," I said. "My Dad's sick."

"OK."

"You think your Mom'll be back soon?"

He shrugged again. "Sometimes she's out late. I never know. She leaves me food and a little money."

"Really?"

"Yeah."

I didn't know what to say. "Don't tell her I stopped by."

"Why not."

"It's just between us guys. She wouldn't get it."

He smiled. "OK."

"It was good hanging out."

"Yeah."

He was sullen again, not looking at me. He was a lonely kid. I knew how it felt. I wanted to say something that would help him feel better, but I didn't know if there was anything I could say that would be true. I was doing the best thing for him, for Anna. For the first time, maybe I was doing something for someone else. There was a strange sensation in my chest, a tightness, but it felt good. I held onto that as I got back in the van and drove away.

CHAPTER 13

It was mid-afternoon and the traffic at Boulder's had subsided. I made it back to the hill and found Dad still sleeping, but his breathing didn't seem right. His breaths were jerky, uneven. My fingers tingled. My heart went light in my chest. I shook him to try to wake him, and his eyes opened a little and all I saw were the whites. I didn't know what to do. I sat down on the floor beside his bed and watched him until it got dark. Each fitful breath he took seemed like it would be his last. I filled the heater, put the groceries away and ate a peanut butter sandwich. The food calmed me a little. I wanted a drink. I wanted to take him to the hospital again and I wanted to drink my face off while someone else took care of him. But I couldn't do that. This was the end and it was my job to be here and preside over it. And I would. And I would be sober while I did it. I sat at the table and watched him in the glow from the stove. I wanted to see the last moment and I was pretty sure it would come soon. I paced around the camper. Hours passed. I sat on the floor again. It was cooler there with the heater going and I wanted to stay awake. I fell asleep after a while.

I woke as the sky silvered with the first light. There was another pain in my neck from sleeping sitting up. I panicked. I feared he was gone. But I saw him there, eyes open, looking at me. He was breathing still, looking right at me, but he wasn't seeing me. His mouth was moving but I could only hear wet raspiness coming from his throat. I went to him and looked in his eyes. They didn't see me. I put my ear close to his mouth, but I couldn't make out any words. I shook his shoulder and his eyes rolled back into his head. When they came back again he saw me.

"John," he said.

"Yeah, Dad, I'm here."

"Hurting bad."

"I got more pills." I shook two out of the bottle and helped him get them down. The water woke him up a little and his eyes cleared.

"I thought I lost you there last night," I said. "You weren't coming around."

"I had a dream. All of us together." He tried to shift in the bed and the pain stopped him.

A gun went off somewhere deep in the forest.

"They're coming for us," he said. His eyes shifted around fast, scared. "Don't let them take me off this hill."

"No, Dad, it's deer season. Started yesterday. There are hunters in the woods."

He opened and closed his mouth a few times. He looked a little like a fish out of water, slowly dying. Was he getting air anymore?

"I want to go hunting," he said.

"I don't think that's going to happen."

He tried to move again. "I'm going to go. I'm hungry. I want deer." He braced his arm under himself and started to slide off the bed. I caught him and put him back under the covers. He freed his arm and reached for the back wall of the camper. I pulled his arm back and pinned it under the blanket.

"Stay still, Dad. You're going to hurt yourself."

"Get me the gun."

"You're not going anywhere. You're staying in bed."

His eyes were wild and filmed over. I wasn't sure if he even knew I was there. I was more scared than I'd ever been.

"Give me the goddamn gun." He raised his voice above a whisper for the first time in days and it brought on a coughing fit. I could hear the wet inside his lungs.

"Where is it?" I said.

"Back there." He motioned to the edge of the bed.

I reached over him and felt between the mattress and the wall. My fingers touched the cold metal and I pulled it out.

I expected the dark, well-worn wood of his rifle, the blue-black of that old weapon. Instead I saw the lighter wood of my own gun, the one he had sold. I knew it was mine immediately.

"I thought you sold this," I said.

"Did. Worst thing I ever did. I was wrong to do that. That was your gun. Wasn't mine to sell."

I held the gun across my lap. "Thank you." I said. I wanted nothing less and nothing more in the world than to have that gun. I hated it. It frightened me, but it was his gift.

The pills had started to work. His eyes were clearer. He managed to get himself half way into a sitting position. "I'm going out," he said.

"No, you're not." I put my hand on his shoulder and held him down.

"I want a deer steak. One last time. My last meal." He tried to stand and I let him. He legs wouldn't hold him and he crumbled back onto the bed. He started weeping. I had never seen him cry before. Fat tears rolled through the crevices of his withered cheeks. He curled into a ball and held his face, hiding from me.

"I'll go," I said. "I'll try and get you a deer."

He reached out and grabbed my arm. He squeezed it hard.

Outside, the air felt colder. The wind was up and it cut through me. I held the rifle in both hands and worked the lever back. It was loaded, the safety on. I hadn't touched a gun since that first hunting day. It still felt good in my hands. I took in a deep breath of the new winter air and my eyes cleared. I put the rifle to my shoulder and sighted the way he had shown me. I took a bead on a piece of rusted metal sticking up out of the cabin foundation and pretended to fire. I could do this. I said that to myself over and over.

I needed a knife. I went to the truck and found Dad's old hunting knife in the glove compartment, right where it had been when I was young. I took it from the sheath and tested the blade on my forearm. Blood popped up and I sucked it away.

I entered the forest on the same place where I saw the deer family. Once under the tree cover, I had to force myself to take deep breaths and calm down. My heart fluttered in my chest. I rested the gun in the crook of my arm and followed the path. There was no sign of the deer left. I tried not to think about what I was doing. I struggled against the vision of myself as a twelve year old, the pressure of the knife—the same knife now in my pocket—against the coarse fur of the deer, the slicing sound it made as it cut through the skin, the spray of blood. I swallowed hard and started down the hill. I moved slow, willing myself to do the job.

At the belly of the hollow, I stopped to catch my breath. My hands felt hot and thick despite the cold and I dipped them in the crick. A mistake. The water was so cold it burned my fingers, but it soothed my cuts. I scanned the woods around me, looking and not looking as I'd been taught. Nothing. Somewhere far away, another shot echoed through the forest. I could be shot. People got shot in the woods hunting every year. I moved on, up the next hill, slow, scanning, looking and not looking. I wanted it to be over.

I walked that way for more than an hour and came to a group of boulders that formed a cave. I sat in the mouth of the cave and let the gun rest across my lap. I knew at that moment I couldn't shoot a deer. A buck could walk right up to me and put its head to the barrel of the rifle and I couldn't pull the trigger. It wasn't in me. But I had to try. I stood and walked further up the hill, past the place where I'd been the day before, toward the clearing above. It was an unknown place. Maybe unknown things could happen there.

The field opened out and rose to a knob of rock a half mile from where I broke through the thicket. I walked through dead knee-high thistle to this highest point. All around me the mountains rose and I couldn't see where they ended. They climbed to the sky and I thought if I were to keep going I could walk into heaven. I stood there for a long time, rifle dangling loose from my right hand, head tilted back, turning, eyes open, living in the white sky.

When I brought my face down again there was a white buck standing fifty yards away, just outside of the tree line. I looked at his rack and tried to count the points—twelve, maybe more. It was too far away to tell. I thought I could just see the mark of a wound on his hindquarter. It stood there for a second—the most beautiful animal I'd ever seen, stark against the green on the virgin hemlock behind it. I had to try to take the shot. I lifted the rifle, sure the deer would spook and be gone.

Rifle to my shoulder, I held it tight and sighted down

the barrel, all as though I'd done this yesterday and not twenty years ago. I thumbed the safety off, drew in a slow, deep breath and held it. My finger caressed the trigger, just barely. *I won't shoot,* I said to myself. Dad in the camper dying, maybe dead. The organs of that long ago deer warming my hands. The knife. The smell of blood and moss.

I squeezed. The shot rang against the hill. The white deer leapt high and disappeared into the hemlock.

I stared at the gun. I had done it. I wasn't going to shoot. But I did shoot. I laid the rifle on the ground and walked to the place where the deer had been. The sky above. The world was unknown. I dropped to my knees and felt around in the brush, checking my hands for blood. I crawled over a twenty-foot square space and found nothing. I missed. Relief. I put my face on the cold ground and cried.

I walked into the hemlock. It was dark under the thick green cover, almost night. My eyes couldn't adjust in the half-light. They struggled for focus. I looked deep into the forest. The deer stood between two thin boughs looking at me. We looked at each other. For a long time it was just the two of us, staring, both a part of the woods. I took a step toward him. The soft dead pine beneath my feet whispered. I closed half the distance between us and he waited for me to come. I said, "Go," and the deer leapt into the brush and was gone.

I walked back to where I left the gun and retrieved it. I crossed the field to the trees without looking back. I was leaving something behind, but I wasn't sure yet what. I entered the trees on the other side of the field floating, free.

It took a long time to get back to the camper. The sun was a white yolk in the sky high above my head when I did. It provided no warmth.

I put the rifle in the truck. I was afraid Dad would know somehow I hadn't killed a deer with it if I brought it into the camper. Dad was where I left him. He heard me come in and stirred.

"Did you get one?" he said. His eyes were wet and glassy. He was in pain again.

I didn't know what to say. I looked at him for a long time.

"Yeah, I got one," I said. "A big one. Twelve point."

"Good. I knew you would."

I shook another two pills out and fed them to him.

"You want to try and eat something. I got some crackers."

He shook his head.

"We'll have deer steaks for supper," I said.

He patted me on the hand and closed his eyes.

I drove to Boulder's. There were a couple trucks with deer in the back and Boulder was checking them in. When he was done I went over to a guy who had two small bucks in the bed of his F-150.

"I'll give you fifty bucks for two deer steaks," I said.

He raised his eyebrows. "Show me the money," he said.

I looked from the man to the deer and back again. I didn't have fifty dollars in my wallet. Suddenly, it was all clear to me.

"Hang on a second," I said. I took the gun from the truck and went inside. I told Boulder what happened. He put his hand on my shoulder and tried to find something to say. He didn't.

"I don't have the money," I said, "I'll take whatever you can give me for this." I offered the gun.

"Your dad saved that for you."

"I know. I don't need it."

He looked at me a long time before he punched open the register and counted out two hundred dollars.

"That's too much," I said.

"I'll get that much for it. It's a good gun."

"I don't want charity."

He reached over the counter and squeezed my arm. He didn't let go until I put the money in my pocket.

I followed the hunter back to his house and stood in the door of his shed while he and his buddy strung the two deer up by their hind legs and peeled the skin off them down to the front hooves. The skin turned inside out and hung from the legs. It reminded me of the one-piece pajamas I'd worn as a boy.

There was surprisingly little blood. He cut away two big steaks and wrapped them in butcher paper. He brought them to me hands still bloody, staining the outside of the paper.

"You must want this pretty bad. There's still plenty of season left."

"I don't have a lot of time." I said. I handed him the fifty and thanked him.

"Easiest fifty I ever made," he said.

"Good for you."

I could hear them laughing at me as I walked back to the van.

Town was silent, the hunters were in their garages with their kills or in the bars talking about their near misses and the next day's hunt. It was getting dark. I made my way through the hollow, past Grandmother's house into the deeper darkness of the old woods. The forest accepted me again and I climbed the hill slow.

I built a fire twenty feet or so away from the camper out of boards and tree limbs. I needed something to grill on, so I climbed into the cabin foundation and pulled the wire rack out of the rusting old stove laying on its side deep in the hole. I was glad it was cold enough that there probably weren't any snakes. I used a little kerosene to get the fire going and then pulled four cinderblocks off the foundation itself and positioned them at four corners around the fire. When the blaze died down, I placed the oven rack over the fire and unwrapped the steaks.

Dad was asleep in the camper, but I cracked the door so if he woke up he could see the fire. He wasn't breathing so well. I made myself busy to keep from thinking about him. I put the steaks on and went inside to set out a couple paper plates. There wasn't much to make a meal out of, so I put some crackers on the plates and some chili. There was no utensil I could use to turn the steaks, so I whittled a long stick to a point and stabbed at them until I got them both flipped. It didn't take long for them to cook. I brought them inside and put them on the plates. I shook Dad awake. His eyes half opened. He mouthed something. I couldn't make it out.

"Supper's ready, Dad."

His eyes widened and I helped him sit up. I gave him two more pills and he sipped at the water while I cut his steak into tiny pieces, like he was a child. I fed him a piece and he chewed on it. After a long time he was able to swallow.

"That's good," he said.

I fed him a few more pieces and a forkful of chili and then he held his hand up.

"I'm full. Thank you. That was good." He smiled.

"You only had a few pieces," I said. "You need to eat something."

"I can't."

"You want to lie down?"

He nodded and I helped him down.

He said, "I'm going to sleep now. Will you do something for me?"

"Sure," I said, "anything."

"In the morning will you play me a song? I want to hear you sing."

My guitar was in the van at the bottom of the hill, but I would do something without it.

"Yeah, Dad. I'll sing for you. Whatever you want. I'll do it now."

"In the morning. I'm gonna sleep now. Thank you." He was asleep soon, or at least he seemed to be asleep. His face was peaceful. His chest rose and fell, even but shallow.

I ate my steak sitting in the camper doorway looking out over the field. It was quiet except the crackle of the fire. The meat was hard for me to eat. I hadn't had deer meat since that day when I was twelve. After that day, I couldn't stand the thought of eating it. But I wanted to eat the steak. It was tough and tasted wild, the way I remembered. I'd cooked it too long and it was dry, but I stuck my fork into the center and gnawed at it until it was gone. I washed it down with spring water.

I drank what was left in the gallon jug and then walked in the dark to the spring and refilled it. I drank half the jug again. I couldn't get rid of the thirst. Finally, my belly distended from all the liquid, I walked back to the camper and watched the fire die. Every so often I looked in and checked Dad's breathing. It would be soon now. I was ready. I came inside and closed the door. I lit the kerosene stove and took my place on the bench seat at the table, leaning against the wall, legs out in the walkway, watching him. I could just see the rise and fall of the blankets.

CHAPTER 14

I slept on and off. A few times in the night I woke and thought I heard him calling my name. Each time I woke, I whispered "Dad," but he didn't answer. The quilts continued to rise and fall as before. I leaned against the wall and drifted off again.

I opened my eyes in the early morning feeling refreshed. I slept deeply those last few hours and my head was clear. I looked at Dad and knew he was dead. Something was gone from his face. It was still the same waxy pale, but the muscles had gone slack and the skin was just a shroud of leather over his skull. I shook all over, panicking. I went to the bed and felt his cheek. It was cool, almost spongy to the touch. His eyes were open just a little. I could see the whites. My stomach tightened and I thought I was going to be sick. I swallowed. My mouth watered. I went to the door and gulped down the cold morning air. I chewed on my tongue until I tasted blood and then I went back to him.

"Dad," I said. Nothing.

I sat on the floor of the camper with one hand resting on the quilts. I didn't know what to do. I wandered outside, into the field toward the tree line. I almost broke into a run but held myself back. I pounded my fist into my thigh. I went to my knees in the middle of the field and said over and over, "You sonofabitch, you sonofabitch, you sonofabitch."

I walked the circumference of the field, studying all the places I knew as a boy, the nooks that seemed too small to me now. I came to the spring. I cupped my hand in the flow and drank and when I had my fill, I ladled the water over my head, down my face and into my shirtfront. It was cold, but felt good. I continued on down the hill. At the creek in the hollow I stepped over on the same rocks we'd used to cross that day we went hunting together. I could still hear him talking to me, telling me what to do, how to do it. He had taught me a lot, but it never seemed like he taught me anything. I could feel him start to change in my mind now that he was gone.

Where was I going? I passed the place where I shot the deer that day, the place where we chased him up the hill was indiscernible. I walked the road headed out of the woods. Was I leaving? Yes. I thought I was. I was already beginning to feel free. I got in the van and started the engine. I listened to it run, waited for the heat to come. It would take a while, but I was willing to wait. So cold. After a few minutes, the vents blew warm. I couldn't bring myself to put the thing in gear.

What would become of him up there? Eventually someone would find him. I was shaking again. I couldn't get the image of him lying there under the quilts out of my head. I hadn't sung him his song. I had to do it. I shut off the van and got out. I got the guitar from the back and beneath the case was the backpack with the master tapes of my record that would never be released. Not knowing exactly why, I took the tapes with me. My music was on there, the voice, everything I thought I could be. I wanted to show him. I climbed back up the hill. The tapes were heavy, the guitar in its hard-shell case made the walk difficult. It was after noon by the time I made it back.

I sat with him for a long time. I ate crackers, my stomach too tender for anything else, and asked him what

I should do. "Don't let them take me off this hill," he said the night before. I took the guitar from the case and played him songs, "Blue Suede Shoes," a Waylon song, Bill Withers. It was like the songs were written for that moment. I asked him over and over again what to do and when dusk gave way to dark, I knew.

There wasn't a lot worth keeping in the camper. I folded one of Grandmother's quilts and put it in the backpack with the picture from that Fourth of July, the cassette of me singing "Country Roads." I used the other quilt to cover him. At the last second, I found the courage to close his eyes for him. I sang him another song, one of mine. I breathed it soft, the guitar barely present underneath. After I was done, I listened to the night come. It would be the last time I heard the night on this hill. The moon shone through the window and lit the inside of the camper in white light. I put the guitar in the case. I hoisted the backpack and gathered the tapes in my arms. They were heavy. And then I decided I wouldn't carry them. I didn't need them. I didn't want them anymore. I put them back on the table and walked out of the camper.

It didn't take long for the clothes and trash to get burning good, and once the fire was rolling, I backed away and watched the flames lick up and catch the curtains, black smoke blotting out the fingernail moon just above the trees in the cloudless night sky. The fire got to the kerosene and there was a small explosion. It scared me. I was excited by it. There were too many smells to tell one from the other—plastic, wood, hot metal, flesh. The window over the sink melted, the fire found its way through the roof. Soon there was nothing but the aluminum shell, flames caressing the night sky. I couldn't watch anymore.

I had to leave the truck there. I wanted whoever came to investigate the fire to think that he died alone, an accident. If they didn't look too hard, there would be no reason to think otherwise. It took a long time to walk back down the mountain to the van. When I got there I was exhausted. There were still hours left until morning. I could see the glow of the fire on the mountaintop above. I laid down in the back of the van.

It was full light when I woke. I half expected to see Devault staring at me through the window, ready to haul me in, but I was alone. The emergency vehicles, the rescue workers, they all would have gone up the front side of the hill, if they came at all. That's why this was Dad's hiding spot for his truck in the first place. I climbed into the driver's seat and started the van. I let it idle and got the heater going.

I thought about Anna. I wanted to go to her, but I would honor her wishes. I would let her go. There was the DUI court date but I didn't care. I was never coming back again. I was leaving. I would always be tied to this place, but I was no longer trapped by it. I pulled off the road at the school, still for sale, price reduced. I looked at the gap-toothed building for a long time, almost aglow, lit by the morning sun.

In the eighth grade, we had to take a West Virginia history class. We learned about the Indian tribes that had lived on the land before the settlers came, about how the state became a state during the Civil War, and about the fourteenth colony of Vandalia, the forgotten colony that gave our town its name.

"Imagine," Mrs. Mailey said as she ran her hand south along the map, "how different our history would have been if a place like Vandalia had existed. Just imagine that."

At the edge of town, I turned into the cemetery and drove to where Mom was buried. I looked toward the hill where the camper had burned itself out. The hills were still the same, unchanged. I stood at the foot of Mom's grave and tried to think of what to say. I told her Dad was dead. I told her I was sorry, that I was OK. I would be OK. I didn't know if that was true, but I wanted it to be. I didn't know where I was going or what I would do, but I was coming out of the dark.

Jason T. Lewis

The Fourteenth Colony

This book also has a companion album of music available for download @ www.sadironpress.com.